"I would like to leave."

"You agreed you'd stay here for two weeks."

"I agreed to nothing," she pointed out tartly.
"You insisted, threatened, in fact. And if I'm
leaving, then why don't you ask yourself whose
fault that is?"

"You'll stay right here."

"What's the point? You'd thrown the press off the
scent even before we came here—so that excuse won't hold water. You only wanted me here
to seduce me." She closed her eyes briefly. "I
won't be your mistress."

DIANA HAMILTON is a true romantic and fell in love with her husband at first sight. They still live in the fairy-tale Tudor house where they raised their three children. Now the idyll is shared with eight rescued cats and a puppy. But despite an often chaotic life-style, Diana has always had her nose in a book—either reading or writing one!

Books by Diana Hamilton

HARLEQUIN PRESENTS
1377—PASSIONATE AWAKENING
1449—AN INCONVENIENT MARRIAGE
1507—THE DEVIL HIS DUE
1548—GAMES FOR SOPHISTICATES
1563—TROUBLESHOOTER
1588—SAVAGE OBSESSION

HARLEQUIN ROMANCE
2865—IMPULSIVE ATTRACTION
2959—PAINTED LADY
2979—THE WILD SIDE

DIANA HAMILTON

A Honeyed Seduction

Harlequin Books

TORONTO • NEW YORK • LONDON
AMSTERDAM • PARIS • SYDNEY • HAMBURG
STOCKHOLM • ATHENS • TOKYO • MILAN
MADRID • WARSAW • BUDAPEST • AUCKLAND

ISBN 0-373-11612-8

A HONEYED SEDUCTION

Copyright © 1992 by Diana Hamilton.

CHAPTER ONE

'It's a honey,' Jake Preston, the gangling head of the film crew asserted as the last of the series of six Favorisi perfume commercials faded from the video screen. 'You're going to be flavour of the month when their directors view this little lot tomorrow!'

'I hope you're right.' Chelsea smiled rigidly, hoping that her abstraction didn't show. It was difficult to concentrate on anything when her mind was seething with rage, when she felt, for perhaps the first time in her life, so damned impotent.

Adding the exclusive Favorisi perfumes to the growing list of clients she had built up for Triple A—as the Avery Advertising Agency was commonly known—had been a major feather in her working cap and had to say something for her drive and ambition, her dedication to her job.

But little things like the ability to live life in the fast lane, always under constant pressure as she set schedules, made sure deadlines were met, talked, argued, ensured the team worked within fairly rigid financial parameters, commissioned market research, hunted out new clients, didn't count for much when it came down to basics, she thought grittily, almost leaping out of her skin when a secretary put her head round the tiny viewing-room door and told her, 'Phone for you, Miss Viner. Your boss.'

'I'll take it in Reception.' She refused to go back to her office. It adjoined Miles Robartes's and if she set eyes on him again today she would kill him. It would be as much as she could do to speak to him.

'You might as well go home now,' she heard him say, wondering why, until this afternoon, she had never detected the oily note in his voice. 'Don't forget our date. I want you looking your divine best at the Ryder-Gem party tonight. The top guy will be there—and they don't come higher than the sole owner and chairman of that particular set-up——'

'It will be a total waste of time,' she cut in snappily, expressing the view she had tossed at him a couple of days ago when he'd first told her they would be attending the launch party for the new 'Manhattan' range of exclusive and, no doubt, fabulously expensive jewellery. But the bones of the hand that gripped the receiver were tight now and there wasn't a vestige of colour in her normally pale skin.

The last thing she wanted was to be around Miles until she'd had time to get her head together and work out how to respond to the utterly distasteful suggestion he'd made this afternoon.

'No, it won't,' he countered peevishly. 'Ryder-Gem handle their own advertising in-house, and we've all heard the whispers about the top-level weed-out in that department. It's bound to leave gaping holes. My hunch is that the whole ad. edifice is tottering and it could be, just could be, that the board will decide to shut down the department and shop around for an independent agency. And if they do I want Triple A to be right there, in the front line. Besides, I sweated blood to get the invites.'

If he was right, and he could be, then their appearance at this evening's function would make sense. And although the last thing she wanted was to spend a major part of the coming evening with her immediate boss she knew she would have to because she couldn't afford to give him the smallest black mark to hold against her.

'We could have dinner afterwards,' he was saying, sounding too smooth and sure of himself, 'and we could discuss the little arrangement I suggested earlier on, couldn't we? That should be fun. I'll pick you up at six-thirty.'

She could hear him licking his lips and her stomach curled in distaste, and she said with heavy and pointed politeness, 'There's no need. I'll make my own way and see you there,' and put the receiver down with a jolt.

Leaving early, as Miles had suggested, wouldn't do any harm, she thought, collecting her briefcase from the viewing-room. She was too incensed to concentrate on anything and the extra time on her own would give her the opportunity to decide how best to turn Miles Robartes's insulting suggestion down flat—without antagonising him too completely, because she couldn't afford to do that, no matter how much she would like to.

June sunlight radiated off the London pavements as she exited from the glass and steel skyscraper where Triple A occupied two whole floors. And a ten-minute walk brought her to the new docklands development, a relatively peaceful riverside oasis in the heart of the teeming city.

She had covered the distance between work and home in record time. She was tall for a girl, and her long stride had helped, despite the narrowness of the skirt of her sage-green linen suit, the height of her spiky heels. She was too tense, too rigid, she recognised, feeling her breath burn in her lungs as her anger translated itself to adrenalin-fuelled energy.

Perspiration beaded her pale forehead where the midnight silkiness of her long black hair was pulled back from her face, secured in the neat chignon she preferred. And the tension that gripped every muscle of her greyhound-slim body was like a greedy hand.

Knowing she had to try to relax, she made herself linger, her deep blue eyes focusing on the gleaming paintwork of the motor launches moored to private landing stages, the tiny wavelets of the Thames glinting against the hulls. Gulls wheeled overhead, reminding her of a long-ago holiday at the coast, before her parents had split up for the last time. But she pushed that thought away with characteristic determination and strode across the paving setts towards the prestigious, brand new building where she lived, practically mortgaging her soul to pay for a small but luxurious studio apartment on the third floor.

If she told Miles Robartes exactly what he could do with his 'little arrangement' she could kiss goodbye to all this, she thought edgily as she returned the security guard's friendly greeting, her high heels clipping on the smooth marble floor as she passed the small exclusive shops and the coffee-house on the ground floor, making for the lifts.

Miles had made it his business to ingratiate himself with the old-fashioned chairman of Triple A; he would only need to whisper a few well-chosen words in the venerable ear to have her demoted—or fired.

Grinding her teeth, she waited while the lift came up from the basement, and as the doors whispered open with a swish of satin-finished metal the sole occupant greeted, 'Hi, gorgeous—when are you going to let me teach you the rudiments of the game?'

He was talking about squash, at least he'd better be, she decided, warming to the humour in the glowing amber eyes.

'Too energetic for me, Quinn,' she dismissed with a slight smile as she entered the lift and the doors closed behind her, locking them in. He was obviously coming up from the large, superbly equipped sports complex in the basement and, if she hadn't been immune to men, Chelsea might have found the way the brief shorts and body-clipping T-shirt he was wearing, revealing the hard muscles of a lean, whippy body that emanated the dangerous hint of carefully leashed strength, too disturbing for her peace of mind.

'Play with me, poppet, and you'll find it more relaxing than exhausting, I promise,' he countered with the lazy smile that revealed hard white teeth, the amber eyes, fringed with curling lashes the exact colour of his closely cropped sable hair, drifting with open assessment over her neatly clad body.

He was still talking about squash; of course he was. He was the type who would prefer lush little blondes, preferably with cotton wool between their ears. He wouldn't try to chat up women who lived for their careers, highly motivated females, clad in expertly tailored, understated suits! He was too darn casual, too laid-back, a whole universe apart from the ruthless males she encountered daily in her career.

His careless insouciance was the very thing that made him easy to talk to. Not that she'd had very much to do with him, she thought quickly, wondering why she suddenly felt far too aware of him for comfort. It was his far superior height and breadth, in a confined space, she rationalised, shaking her head as he invited, 'Come on up and have a coffee—or something long and cold, if you prefer?'

They'd had coffee together once, in the ground floor restaurant one Sunday morning a couple of weeks ago. They'd been the only two availing themselves of the heated pool in the sports complex, had got talking, and it had been easy to fall in with his suggestion that they continue their conversation over coffee and croissants. But now she shook her head.

'I've got too much on. Some other time, maybe.' And breathed an unwarranted sigh of relief as the lift stopped on her floor.

She deliberately avoided his eyes as she scampered out and only when she was safely in her own apartment did she berate herself for the slowness of her wits.

It wasn't like her to miss such an opportunity, she grumbled at herself as she walked to the bedroom and kicked off her shoes. Coincidentally, the penthouse belonged to Ryder-Gem, the international, long-established jewellery house, kept for the sole purpose of providing superb and centrally situated accommodation for visiting overseas business associates—or so it was rumoured.

And Quinn—she had never learned his surname—had been occupying it, on and off, for the past two or three weeks. He was certainly no foreign buyer or trader in precious stones, and her best guess was that he had some connection with the Ryder family—probably the black sheep, more than content to live off the back of the privately owned company. A family whose wealth and success was as legendary as the Ryders' could afford one black sheep, she thought acidly, stripping off and padding through to the elegantly appointed bathroom.

And if that was the case, and she had a shrewd suspicion it was, then she should have taken up his offer of a drink and pumped him for information on the rumoured disbandment of Ryder-Gem's advertising department. Miles had got wind of it, which was why he had been so keen that they put up a showing this evening at the party to launch the new 'Manhattan' range of jewellery created by the firm's design department. Someone as laid-back and casual as Quinn wouldn't have had any scruples about discussing business matters which a more concerned and involved family member would have kept to himself.

But, she excused herself as she stood gratefully under the refreshing needles of water, she had been too disturbed by the events of the afternoon to think clearly or concisely to take up the opportunity Quinn had offered. She had achieved her present position with Triple A— PA to the television director—through her own hard work, her dedication to her career. It had come as a shock of the most appalling kind to learn that she would go no further unless she agreed to share Miles Robartes's bed!

Two hours later she was no nearer finding the solution to her problem and she was livid with herself as she paid off the taxi outside the famous London hotel where the Ryder-Gem launch party was being held.

Aggravatingly, her mind had been too occupied with the missed opportunity Quinn had so casually offered to allow her to search for a solution to a very tricky situation.

Her face set, she scanned the board in Reception and mounted the wide stairs to the appropriate room, ignoring the lifts because she needed time to think. She'd worked with Miles Robartes for two years and she'd learned a lot from him about the making of commercials, and she'd been grateful for the opportunities he'd given her, grasping them with both hands and making more of them for herself, finding herself, latterly, practically running the department.

She had never liked him on a personal level because, even before his divorce, he had made no secret of his affairs, but that hadn't meant she hadn't been able to work with him. And when he'd told her, only this morning, that he was moving on and up, to head the expanding documentaries department, she had asked him if he would recommend her to the chairman for the vacancy his own promotion would create.

Without conceit, she knew she was ready for the challenge, that she was the best person for the job, but she also knew her chairman. Of the old school, he was the quintessential chauvinist. In his view, women didn't reach top positions or achieve board level. And although she knew she was right for the job, had earned it, Chelsea also knew she would need Miles Robartes on her side, putting her case to the chairman in no uncertain terms.

Trouble was, Miles knew it too. And yes, he had agreed; he could think of no one better suited to step into his shoes, and he would certainly press that point to the chairman, and he could swing it, too. Providing…

Chelsea's face flamed with unaccustomed colour as she slipped into the luxurious powder-room and waited while her rage abated. If the only way to gain the promotion she knew she deserved was to go to bed with Miles Robartes, then she would rather be out on her neck!

But even while she had faced him, itching to slap his jowled face, the logical part of her brain had told her that there had to be another way. A way to make him withdraw his disgusting proviso without leaving him antagonistic enough to ruin her chances for promotion forever.

The way, however, completely eluded her.

Suddenly conscious that she had been unseeingly staring into the rose-tinted mirror for longer than she dared contemplate, she blinked rapidly and dragged in a deep breath, noting with neither approval nor vanity that the sleekly styled black cocktail dress she was wearing made her look coolly sophisticated, the deeply slashed V neckline emphasising the slender length of her neck, the hemline—just above her knees—performing the same service for her legs.

Consciously letting go of the anxious frown-line between her slightly slanting, blackly fringed deep blue eyes, she straightened her shoulders. She would endure the party, Miles's company, for the next hour, because she had no option. But later she would tell him that she had no intention of sharing his bed, would approach the chairman herself—taking care to lobby the other members of the board beforehand—and take her chances.

It would dent his over-blown ego, she was fully aware of that. And she knew, from past observations, that he could be spiteful. She wouldn't put it past him to go straight to the top and complain about her work, making sure she never got promotion, she thought despairingly as she walked down the corridor. But, since she hadn't been able to think of a way to turn him down without making him feel a fool, she would just have to grit her teeth and hope for the best.

Pinning an empty smile on her face, she approached the open doors to the reception-room. There was piped music, unobtrusive, muted conversation, most eyes glued to the willowy model girls wearing the gems that made up the new 'Manhattan' collection, and Chelsea's stomach gave a sickening lurch as she picked out Miles Robartes's stocky figure and iron-grey head, saw the flicker of a leer in his eyes as he turned and saw her in the doorway.

She should never have asked him to recommend her, she cursed herself uselessly. But, knowing of the chairman's blind spot where women employees were concerned, she had believed her request made sense. She would never have imagined in a million years that he would have turned round and told her, 'I've fancied you rotten ever since you joined me. But I know when I'm up against an iceberg. I've always hoped I'd find a way to melt you, so try this on for size—I'll recommend you, in the strongest terms, and I'll come up with the goods, believe me, because I won't have to lie, you are the bloody best. And in return you'll warm my bed for exactly as long as I want you there. Turn me down and I'll put in a word, all right. Only it will be the kind that gets you slung out on your elegant neck—with the sort of reference that would make you unemployable in the same field.'

And he'd do it, she knew he would, and no one, least of all the chairman, would take her word against his. And if she'd been able to think of a way out of this, something that would make him retract his threats, make him back off without a loss of face, she would be one mightily relieved woman.

But she hadn't, and tension coiled bitingly in her stomach as she watched him make his way towards her. He was carrying a glass of champagne in one hand and he took another, for her, presumably, from one of the white-coated waiters who were circulating among the guests—the rich and the beautiful—and the security guards who stuck out like sore thumbs.

If she swallowed as much as one drop she would be ill. And she knew that she had to tell him what he could do with his 'arrangement' straight away. She could no more endure a moment in his company than sit, stark naked, on a bed of hot coals!

And then she saw Quinn across the room and her heart gave a crazy leap. And she thought, Why not? Why, in the sweet name of madness, not?

He was looking, for him, extraordinarily suave, his elegantly tailored black dinner suit lending him an indefinable aura of authority. She had to bite down hard on the full softness of her lower lip to quell the bubble of laughter that was building up inside her. As a hanger-on he had probably come along for the free champagne and delicious fork-food and, give him another half an hour, and his perfectly tied necktie would be coming adrift and he would be chatting up the nearest luscious lovely! But, for now, he looked perfectly sober—a rather commanding figure if one hadn't got to know him in his true colours: sybaritic, laid-back, a smooth-tongued playboy with no hang-ups about sponging on others.

But he would do, he would do perfectly! She knew, from her former conversations with him, that he had a finely honed sense of humour, and, if she was any judge of character at all, he wouldn't be averse to playing along.

'I thought you weren't going to show.' Miles had at last made it to her side and, because she had at last figured a way out of the spot he had put her in, she was able to look at him without actually spitting in his eye. 'But I might have known you'd got more sense than that,' he continued complacently. 'You haven't got as far as you have with Triple A by being stupid.' His watery eyes were on her cleavage and, if she hadn't spotted Quinn, this was where she would have been telling him a few well chosen home-truths. But, studiously ignoring the glass of champagne he was holding out to her, only half listening to his self-important, 'I haven't wasted any time. I reckon my hunch was right and I've been dropping a few words about the agency in the right quarter,' Chelsea butted in,

'Please excuse me for a moment, Miles. And, before you say any more on the subject you broached this afternoon, there's someone I'd like you to meet.' And swayed away, moving through the crowd.

Her words had been sweetly said, and she felt sweet. Sweet and light with relief, buoyant with the certainty that she was taking him on, playing him at his own game—and winning. Or about to!

Fixing her eyes on Quinn as she eased her way through the guests, she revised her estimate of his age. On the few brief occasions when they had previously met she'd put him at around twenty-eight, a couple of years her senior. But seeing him now, deeply engrossed in what appeared to be a serious conversation, she noted an air of toughness about his face, a face that was more compellingly attractive than conventionally handsome. Toughness where she would have expected smooth urbanity, an impression of hard authority that made her reassess his age to the mid-thirties mark.

Not that it mattered, of course, and she gave a tiny sigh of relief when she saw him break away from the group he'd been with, because now she wouldn't have to muscle in on a private conversation, and she said his name—'Quinn'—and he turned slowly, his eyes blank at first then warming, lazily appreciative lights glinting deep in the glowing amber gaze.

'Chelsea—you've made my evening! Dare I hope you followed me here, or would that be classed as presumption?' His smile was utterly devastating. For a moment the megawatt force of it took her breath away, but only for a moment, and her answering grin was wide because he was back to being the casual, lightweight charmer of her hitherto slight acquaintance.

That momentary impression of danger, of a toughness of character she had been unable to equate with her small knowledge of him, had been nothing more than a wild fancy.

And she said, for some unknown reason sounding breathless, 'Would you do me a huge favour?' then faltered, wondering if her brainwave had been as brilliant as she'd first believed as she watched his eyes darken with narrow-eyed speculation, his smile tightening with something that looked remarkably like wary distaste.

But she pulled herself together. She had nothing to lose, he could always tell her to get lost, and her idea—if questionable—was the only one she had. Besides, her career was on the line, and her career was the only thing she had. She had made it her life and it was worth fighting for, even if the strategy was devious!

All around them the conversation level was rising as the champagne flowed freely, punctuated by the fizz of flashlight as the invited Press members photographed the models, lights glittering back from the fabulous gems that adorned graceful necks and bone-slender wrists.

Reminding herself that he was the kind of joker who wouldn't turn a hair at the type of deception she was about to suggest, that playing along—even if only for a few moments—would enliven what had to be the boredom of the type of goalless life he led, she continued belatedly,

'Would you mind pretending to be engaged to me? Make out the wedding's to take place very shortly—just while I introduce you to my boss back there?' And saw the shutters come down over his eyes completely, making her feel as if she was looking at a blank page, and this wasn't the reaction she had expected at all. She'd expected a grinning compliance, a boyish eagerness to play games. In fact, she'd banked on it, she realised in retrospect, knowing that being introduced to her 'fiancé', a man much younger, physically far more powerful than he, would have been the one way Miles Robartes could have been persuaded to back off without losing face. If he could have been made to believe she was deeply in love and about to be married, her spurning of his 'arrangement' wouldn't have dented his ego too badly.

Not that she cared about Robartes's hateful ego, of course; it could be flattened for all she cared. But she did care about the depth of his spite if he did as he'd threatened and put her firmly in the chairman's black books.

'Please,' she uttered huskily, bracing herself for one last try. 'It is important, and you'd only have to pretend for a couple of minutes. I'd be very grateful.'

She wished she'd never got herself into this, she thought distractedly, flustered by the way Quinn's eyes came back to life, wickedly drifting over the svelte lines of her body, lifting again to linger on the full pout of her mouth as his own curved sinfully.

'How grateful are you prepared to be, I wonder?' One strongly marked black brow lifted tauntingly and Chelsea gulped, thrown off guard and not knowing what to do about it. Not knowing how to counter the unprecedented *frisson* of entirely unwelcome sensation that flooded through her as he placed an arm around her shoulders, the pads of his fingers intimately caressing the bare flesh of her upper arm.

'Relax, gorgeous,' he commanded softly. 'If it's that important to you, I'm willing to run with your idea. So lead me to the guy, but be warned—as an about-to-be-married man I come into the deeply loving category.' His eyes were now molten gold, mesmeric, and she got the crazy, illogical feeling that she had hurled herself out of the frying-pan, deep into the hottest part of the fire, and that impression deepened terrifyingly when he laid his lips against her ear and whispered, 'And I shall demand reciprocation on your part, my lovely, when you display all that promised gratitude!'

CHAPTER TWO

'MARRIED?' Miles echoed on a high thin note. 'Nobody told me you were engaged to be married!'

He looked as though he'd just been told the earth was flat—incredulous was too weak a word, Chelsea decided grimly. It was almost as if he'd seen straight through the charade, and something would have to be said or done to convince him. And she was knotting her brain, trying to fathom out what she could say to wipe that look of disbelief from his jowly face, when Quinn took matters out of her hands and stated huskily, and, to her mind, far too loudly, 'Very much so. And very soon. I can't wait.' And he drew her closer to the length of his whippy, power-packed body, using his other hand to tilt her chin and gaze deep into her wary eyes. 'Neither of us can, that's right, isn't it, my darling?'

And what was she expected to say to that? she thought crossly, heatedly outraged by the way his hand had now dropped from her chin to her waist, an overtly fondling hand, rising slowly and definitely erotically towards the top of her ribs. She felt as if she were about to explode, her face awash with fiery colour. But, given the circumstances, all she could do was ungrit her teeth and agree, her simple affirmative emerging with disgraceful hoarseness.

'Aren't you going to congratulate me on my good fortune, Robartes?' Quinn asked silkily, his one hand dangerously near the soft underswell of her left breast now, the fingers of the other hand tracing trails of sensation over the suddenly sensitised skin of her arm.

For a moment Chelsea was grossly tempted to stamp down hard, driving a spiky heel through his highly polished shoe, but the common sense of which she was so justly proud told her that it would give the game away. Women who were stupidly in love, about to be married, simply didn't do that sort of thing.

And Miles answered Quinn's question woodenly, 'Of course,' and Chelsea experienced a brief upsurge of triumph because her boss would have to believe the lie now and he wouldn't be trying to blackmail her into his bed in future, and then went into immediate panic as one of the other guests, who had obviously overheard the whole conversation, which had been too loudly conducted in Chelsea's view, screeched,

'Is it true? Have you finally decided to tie the knot, Quinn, darling?' She was a woman in her forties, expensively groomed with eyes like lasers. Gimlet-blue lasers, busily assessing Chelsea's face and form, putting a price—probably exact, right down to the last penny—on the dress she was wearing, the modest gold chain around her neck, a matching piece around one wrist.

And then, after the minutest pause of utter silence, pandemonium. And Chelsea stood, in the middle of it all, her stomach sinking down to the soles of her shoes, right in the heart of a noisy nightmare, trapped amid the shaking of hands, the cries of congratulations, the sudden shocks of half a dozen flashlights and the determined questions from the invited journalists.

Stupidly, she was grateful for Quinn's increasingly supportive arm. Without its strength she would have fallen in a heap, bewailing the hornet's nest she had so unthinkingly stirred. Never, in her wildest imaginings, would she have dreamed that a simple lie, told for the benefit of one man only, could have escalated so cataclysmically into what had to be one of the most public announcements ever!

And so she was doubly grateful—though afterwards she would wonder how she could have been so stupid—when Quinn's deeply authoritative voice cut incisively through the hubbub.

'I know you'll all excuse us, but——' the very slightest, almost indiscernible pause '—my fiancée and I have a dinner engagement.'

She wasn't thinking straight as she allowed him to lead her from the room. She felt as if she'd just escaped from a particularly lively three-ringed circus. And when they'd descended to the foyer and he told her lightly, 'I'll have the car brought around. I know somewhere where we'll find a table—I take it you're not averse to eating simply?' the words 'No way, Jose!' sprang to mind.

But, just in time, she swallowed the scathingly ungracious retort. After all, his compliance had enabled her to best Miles Robartes, leaving her, hopefully, free of his vicious brand of retribution. And if Quinn had gone over the top, played his part much too convincingly, she shouldn't complain. He was obviously a sexual opportunist and had taken what he had no doubt deemed well-earned liberties with both hands—quite literally!

But it was over now, she thought with an inner sag of relief, and all she wanted to do was return to her small but beautifully kept apartment, unwind, and work out her tactics for lobbying the more approachable members of the board, because, whatever happened, she was determined to gain the promotion she deserved.

'There's no need, thank you,' she replied instead. 'I'll get a taxi and go straight home.' She didn't know why she was suddenly feeling nervous, so nervous, anyway. She was used to fending off male advances. A single cool look was usually all it took to get the message of complete uninterest through. She manufactured a very polite smile—after all, despite his reprehensible talent for taking liberties, she did owe him something.

'I'm extremely grateful for what you did back there, but I wouldn't dream of dragging you away from the party, or whatever arrangements you'd made for the rest of the evening.'

She felt she had handled that well, but wasn't so sure when his sensuous mouth hardened dramatically, his voice silky with menace, overflowing with confidence as he taunted, 'As gratitude comes, yours is too low-key for my liking. Look on having dinner with me tonight as a down-payment for my part in a charade I'm no nearer understanding now than I was half an hour ago. Besides——' there was the thrust of sharply honed steel behind the silken taunt now '—what's to stop me going straight back up there and announcing that it was all a sham, a particularly juvenile practical joke?'

'Nothing,' she gritted right back, her chin up. She didn't know why she felt so disappointed in him. She hadn't imagined him to be the type to resort to blackmail. Those sort of tactics belonged to the Miles Robartes of this world.

'You saw what a sensation our engagement announcement created.' He smiled without humour. 'Imagine what would happen if I walked back in and said it was all a lie.'

She didn't need too fertile an imagination to see the vicious glint of revenge in Robartes's eyes if he ever learned how she'd tried to make a fool of him, but she wasn't about to allow two men to make threats in one day and she hissed, 'There wouldn't have been such a sensation if you'd kept your mouth shut and your hands to yourself!'

It had begun as a few quiet words, solely for the benefit of Miles Robartes, and, following that, they could have sloped away quietly, to the other side of the room, leaving her hateful boss to nurse his own thwarted ambitions. But no, oh, no! Sexy-pants here had to make a great big production, all roving hands and hot, empty words!

'I never do anything half-heartedly, my lovely. When you get to know me better, you'll realise that.' Quinn's mouth curved with the faintly mocking smile that, for some reason or other, always made her feel overheated, and she clutched her ribbed silk evening purse until her knuckles showed white. She had no intention of getting to know him better. The occasional casual meeting in the lifts, the coffee-shop or sports complex, the exchange of a few polite, friendly words was as far as their relationship went. Now or ever. But, as if he read his dismissal in her eyes and had no intention of taking it, he uttered blandly, 'I think you owe me an hour of your time. If only to explain what that charade back there was all about.'

'Oh...' Chelsea felt like a pricked balloon. Always fair-minded, she knew he was right. She did owe him that much. And, like it or not, their secret, two-minute 'engagement' had developed into a far too public declaration of intent which, even to someone as light-minded as Quinn, would present a few awkward moments when it came to explaining away the fact that a wedding would never take place.

'Very well, then. Just dinner.' She gave in as gracefully as she could and instantly regretted it when his mouth quirked as he came back,

'I hadn't suggested anything more, but if you're willing so am I.'

And she was still feeling hot all over as a uniformed doorman came to inform him that his car had been brought round to the front and her mouth was set in a very straight line as he handed her into a gleaming BMW.

She would have expected him to drive something less sedate, a spectacular, low-slung, growly sports model, bright red, something more in keeping with his playboy personality, she thought sourly.

She wasn't normally sour, over-critical of others, she recognised with a small sigh. She always kept herself to herself, got on with her life, and allowed others the same privilege.

Her uncharacteristic edginess was down to the way her well-ordered lifestyle had been turned on its head in the space of twelve hours, she consoled herself. She wasn't used to having the neat and direct lines of her carefully planned life muddled by men. Threatening men.

Though, of course, Miles and Quinn were in different leagues. Miles's threats—if she hadn't been able to block them—would have proved disastrous to her career, whereas Quinn's could be discounted.

He wouldn't have carried out his threat to go back to the party and tell everyone that the engagement was a pure fabrication. For one thing he was too insouciant to care, to put himself to that kind of trouble. For another, despite his lazy lifestyle, he was shrewd enough, probably, to protect his own interests.

Had he gone back up, made that threatened statement, he would have caused a commotion of the kind that wouldn't have pleased the august head of the Ryder-Gem empire. He could have found himself turned out of the prestigious penthouse suite much sooner than he'd bargained for.

Come to think of it, she hadn't been introduced to the patriarchal head of the international, world-renowned gem empire. Miles had said he'd been putting a word in for Triple A, and that was as much as she knew. She'd been far too concerned with coming up with a feasible way of explaining to her boss exactly why she couldn't and wouldn't fall in with his hateful blackmailing tactics. And she was confident that she had achieved that objective, so, despite the turmoil of the evening, she had emerged unscathed. And, in spite of a few, merely momentary doubts back there, she had nothing to fear from Quinn.

He had nothing to do with her career, which was the most important thing in her life. If he kept his mouth shut regarding the true nature of their so-called engagement, just for a few days, he wouldn't be able to muddy the waters.

Just a few days—long enough for her to lobby the directors, put her job application in writing to the chairman...she would have to think long and carefully about the wording...

Emerging from her introspection, she realised that Quinn was entering the private underground car park that serviced their apartment block. So he had obviously decided he couldn't be bothered to insist that she have dinner with him and was delivering her home before going on to spend the evening with some other, more impressionable and amenable female. Her earlier impressions of him had been well-founded. He had no staying power; the playboy type never did.

Realising that the sudden drag of disappointment was due to nothing more than a very human regret for the waste of a life—he was powerfully attractive and obviously intelligent and should be able to do more with himself than fritter his undoubted energies away on the mere pursuit of enjoyment—she let herself out of the car, as he did, smiled at him over the gleaming roof, a polite word of thanks hovering on her lips, then widened her eyes as he locked the car and pocketed the key.

So he, too, was having a quiet evening at home, she thought perplexedly, falling in step beside him, making for the lifts. But, she supposed, even the most dedicated playboy had to take the occasional night off from the pursuit of pleasure. And she thought no more about it, allowing him to punch the requisite numbers on the panels, telling herself that the incomprehensible lump of disappointment lodged beneath her breastbone was simply reaction to the uncomfortable turmoil of the past hour or so.

She wasn't really disappointed at the way the evening had ended, the way he'd uninterestedly given up on his stated intention to spend time with her. No, of course she wasn't.

But her earlier nervousness came gushing back as the metal box soared past her floor and came silently to rest at the top of the building. And as the doors hissed open Quinn clamped a hand around her elbow and hustled her out, but she dug her heels into the thick carpeting that covered the foyer at the entrance to the penthouse and grunted, 'Why am I here?' She had her suspicions and he duly confirmed them.

'Somewhere quiet, simple food and an available table,' he replied, and punched numbers on the security panel then stood aside, ushering her over the threshold.

She might have known! He'd never miss a trick; how much quieter could a dinner for two get? She was paying now for her earlier irrational feeling of disappointment, wasn't she just? But she had her pride and she swept ahead of him into the apartment, her head high.

She would have felt much easier if he'd taken her to a crowded restaurant, but she wasn't going to give his ego the fillip that that kind of knowledge would supply. Not that he'd try anything, of course; she assuredly wasn't his type, which left her unable to answer the vexed question of why she was nervous in the first place!

Not that she wanted to answer it, of course; she wasn't that interested, and just to prove that nothing he could do would faze her she glanced around the huge room she found herself in, gave him her most brilliant smile and offered, 'You could fit my apartment into here three times over and still have enough room left over to hold a small party.'

She had her fair share of curiosity and looked around with open interest. Meryl, who worked in the ground-floor coffee-house, and who often hovered to chat when Chelsea indulged in her weakness for croissants and Greek honey on Sunday mornings, had stated that the penthouse was out of this world. And she'd been right, too, Chelsea thought. The careful use of lighting spots gave subtle definition to the casual grouping of comfortable, suede-covered armchairs, fabulous Persian rugs which created brilliant areas of colour, exquisite porcelain displayed on glass shelves which seemed to float against the walls.

Quinn had removed his jacket, loosened his tie, and the flattering cut of his formal black trousers, crisp white shirt, emphasised his alarmingly indolent grace and, because she found her eyes riveted on him as he moved to the far end of the room, sliding back the glass panels that gave on to a balustraded terrace overlooking the Thames, she cleared her throat and remarked crisply, 'You'll miss all this space and luxury when you have to move out. When Ryder-Gem need the apartment.' And saw him swing on his heels, his face momentarily blank before he gave a minimal shrug and that familiar, laid-back grin.

'Come and watch while I throw some food together.' He held out a strong, perfectly formed hand but Chelsea ignored it. Not that it did her much good because he simply reached for one of hers and tugged her along behind him. An alarming shudder of sensation created unwanted havoc in her veins as his fingers closed around hers and she wondered, appalled, if her reaction had somehow transmitted itself to him.

But not, apparently. His face showed nothing. But then, why should it? He was obviously a very physical person; touching would come naturally to him. And, quite probably, if he spent a day without female company of the more intimate kind he would get withdrawal symptoms!

She was far more fastidious, Chelsea reassured herself as she took the high stool he had indicated in the fabulous technological wonder that was the kitchen. Emotional involvements were not for her, and the idea of casual sex was abhorrent, which was why she kept the opposite sex at bay. Which, in turn, was why the unaccustomed touch of a man's warm hand clasping hers had made her feel so peculiar.

Having sorted that out to her own satisfaction, she took the glass of white wine he gave her with a gracious little smile and he gave her a long, level look and stated, 'I hope you're hungry, and not on a diet. I can't stand women who starve themselves because they think it's fashionable to be thin.'

She didn't dignify that remark with a reply, sipped her wine instead. So she was thin. So what? She'd always been able to eat what she liked without gaining an ounce, always remaining greyhound-slender—except for her breasts, which, she considered, were too pronounced for the rest of her.

He would go for curvy, lush blondes, she thought crossly, watching him tie a clean tea-towel around his lean waist. Fluff-heads. It had been Meryl from the coffee-shop who had informed her, before she, Chelsea, had ever set eyes on him,

'The most attractive hunk I've ever laid eyes on is using the penthouse suite. He must be some offshoot of the Ryder family itself; I mean, he isn't a foreign buyer for sure. He's usually got a gorgeous female hanging on his arm—I've seen him with three different ones myself, two blondes and a redhead! He can't work—he wouldn't have time—not with all those women, plus the time he seems to spend in the gym or on the squash courts. You just wait till you see him—he'll knock your eyes out! Make you go weak at the knees and blow your brain!'

And everything Chelsea had noted herself, about Quinn the Charmer, had gone to reinforce Meryl's opinion, except that no man, and certainly not a womaniser who sponged on his family connections, would make her go weak at the knees—or blow her brain!

'So what was that all about?' Quinn asked softly. 'Why was it so important that I agree to pretend to be your fiancé?'

He'd put two herb-sprinkled salmon steaks into a fish-poacher, and now he was dicing aubergines and green peppers and Chelsea disabused him quickly.

'Not you, personally. Any man would have done.' She didn't add that just seeing him at that party had put the idea into her head and that he, of all the men she had ever met, was light-minded enough to take such a crazy suggestion in his stride.

'I stand suitably and thoroughly deflated,' he said, refilling the wine glass she hadn't realised she'd drained. But he didn't look deflated at all, she decided, eyeing him speculatively. She'd met arrogant men, even cocky, strutting men, in the course of her working life, but never one who so effortlessly exuded so much self-assured confidence.

'So?' A dark brow tilted upwards and she resigned herself to telling all because he, more than anyone, did have a right to know.

He didn't interrupt as she talked and she watched as he lightly fried the diced vegetables in olive oil, adding thinly sliced onions and red-wine vinegar. She spoke stiltedly at first and then, because he was such a good listener, she grew more relaxed, and when he piled a tray with the poached salmon, crisp herb bread and aubergine salad and told her, 'Follow me, gorgeous, and bring the bottle and glasses, would you?' she uncrossed her long silk-clad legs and slid down from the stool, still chattering, doing as he'd asked and trotting after him as he took the food to a table on the terrace.

She couldn't remember when she'd last spoken so freely and openly to anyone, she thought with a sense of quiet amazement as she sat facing him, the faint breeze from the river cooling her cheeks, teasing a few tantalising strands of midnight hair from the hitherto severe line of her chignon.

Since childhood she had learned to keep her thoughts and emotions to herself, presenting a calm, unruffled exterior to the world at large, successfully hiding what she really felt until, just lately, there hadn't been anything to hide, no messy emotions, no irrational fears. Nothing. Not even when her sister, Joannie, had poured tears and rage down the telephone. All she, Chelsea, had been able to do was murmur platitudes, carefully holding back the instinctive, 'I told you so. Love doesn't last, so what did you expect?'

No, the only real, gut-twisting emotion she had experienced in ages was today's rage against Miles Robartes. And that, predictably, had been because of her job. Her career at Triple A was the only important thing in her life now.

'The man's obviously a bastard,' Quinn remarked quietly, twisting the stem of his wine glass round in supple, strong fingers. And Chelsea resurfaced from the quiet dark pool of her thoughts, noted the straight line of his mouth, the slight clenching of his black brows, and interpreted his expression as boredom. He would only be comfortable with light chit-chat—preferably spiced with sexual innuendo. He was that type. Anything else would bore him out of his socks.

So she smiled, shrugging, and replied, 'Obviously. But, thanks to your connivance, he'll withdraw his threats. He won't put in a good word for me, but at least he won't have the motive to put in a bad one. I can approach the chairman under my own steam.' It was said with a confidence she didn't actually feel because she knew her chairman, and when Quinn said softly,

'What makes you so sure Robartes will back off?' she had to stiffen her spine against the fluttering of panic because, annoyingly, that scenario had fleetingly and uncomfortably occurred to her. And he went on smoothly, 'If I wanted a woman that badly, no amount of fiancés would put me off.'

'I'm sure they wouldn't!' The words were bitten out before she could stop them and she tacked on gracelessly, 'I'm only surprised you don't actually condone Robartes's attempted blackmail!'

Thick black lashes swept down to hide the gold glitter of his eyes as his gaze lowered to rest on the suddenly vulnerable line of her mouth, and he said silkily, 'I've never yet had to resort to those kind of tactics to get the woman I want into my bed.'

She bit back the furious yet truthful 'I believe you!' just in time, appalled by the way this one man could dredge emotion—albeit angry emotion—from the dark recesses of her psyche where she had, up until now, so successfully relegated it.

Her uncharacteristic outbursts were understandable, she consoled herself, putting her hand over the top of her wine glass as Quinn lifted the bottle towards her with a slight inclination of his beautifully shaped head. They had everything to do with Miles Robartes's hateful suggestions and nothing whatsoever to do with Quinn's raw, smoky sexuality, the indolent grace that made her want to shake him into the realisation that he was wasting his life.

Though why she should bother herself over the profligate waste of his undoubted potential she didn't know. The way he chose to run his life was nothing to do with her, was it?

And after tonight she would not have to have anything more to do with him, beyond a polite word in passing. And there would be a limit to the length of time Ryder-Gem could allow him to laze away his days and nights in idle, womanising luxury at their expense. The penthouse suite would be needed for those foreign clients Meryl had spoken about. And Meryl should know,

Chelsea thought wryly. She had an uncanny knack of discovering all there was to know about the various residents of the block.

Nevertheless, something she had no control over at all made her say, 'Thank you for the delicious meal and the way you helped me at the party. It's a pity you can't channel your obvious talents and energies into something more worthwhile than entertaining females and playing deceptive games.'

Even as the censure emerged she felt a prig. She, who believed wholeheartedly in live-and-let-live, was acting like a prudish maiden aunt. It wasn't like her at all. But then, she had been acting out of character ever since she'd seen him at the party and conceived that wild idea...

She got to her feet with a marked lack of her normal fluidity and reached for her evening purse, anxious to be gone before she said anything else she might regret, but Quinn was on his feet, too, and the steel in his voice told her that he wasn't letting her tactless remark ride. Playboy he might be, but he obviously had some self-respect.

That much was made clear when he reminded her, 'The deception was your idea. And I agreed because, just for a moment, you looked soft and afraid, totally vulnerable.' He gave her a hard look before striding to the door, opening it with a flourish that told her more clearly than any words how he couldn't wait to see the back of her, telling her coldly, 'I have no desire to have my name linked, matrimonially, with yours, believe me. The idea appalls me.'

And that insult hurt more than it had any right to do, Chelsea thought, walking rigidly towards the lift, wondering why her heart was thumping until it actually hurt, why the snick of the penthouse door as he closed it sounded so damnably final, why she felt so suddenly alone . . .

CHAPTER THREE

CHELSEA overslept for the first time ever, surfacing with a strong disinclination to go into work. And that was unprecedented, too, because her job at Triple A was the only thing that made the adrenalin flow.

She simply wasn't looking forward to facing Miles, that was all, she chundered to herself as she fled around the bathroom, more thumbs than fingers this morning and definitely no time for her usual leisurely breakfast of a lightly boiled egg, toast and coffee.

But, facing her mirrored image as she tugged the mid-grey, severely styled suit jacket over the tailored cream blouse she was wearing, she had to admit that her immediate superior at Triple A had nothing to do with her wish to crawl straight back into bed and not emerge until her brain was running on a nice, uneventfully smooth track again.

It was all down to Quinn, wasn't it? she admitted reluctantly. To Quinn and those withering, prissy remarks she had made. To the sudden, urgent and rather ridiculous need she felt to apologise. Apologise?

Hah! She snapped her teeth together as she grabbed her briefcase and let herself out of her apartment, banging the door behind her. Why apologise for speaking the truth?

By the time she had covered half the distance to the agency building she had convinced herself that his uncalled-for remark about being appalled by the idea of having his name linked matrimonially to hers cancelled out her viperish comments regarding his lifestyle.

And by the time she was opening her office door she was back on form, all her mental faculties girded for action and definitely back on track. Quinn meant nothing to her, one way or another; he could say what he liked—anything he liked—and it wouldn't affect her. Why should it? He had been useful and she had been grateful and, until those last few minutes at the end of dinner last night, they had got along fine, and she had explained—because he had earned the right to know—and she had thanked him. And if he hadn't started boasting about his prowess in the seduction stakes, the way he had never, would never have to resort to underhand tactics to get the woman of his fickle fancy into his bed, then that rather degrading slanging match would not have taken place.

Quite why the thought of his sexual expertise should have had that sort of effect on her she wasn't prepared to think about. Not now, not ever. She had more important things to think of. Like Miles Robartes and his reaction to the way she had spiked his guns at the Ryder-Gem party.

And Miles was there, sitting behind her desk, and her chin came up, her eyes very blue, very cool and direct. Adrenalin pumping now because she knew what to say, how to act. She could tell him to get lost without sending him to his friend the chairman, full of sly lies about her lack of efficiency, her mishandling of clients, or other damaging untruths.

He shot to his feet, the ingratiating smile on his face surprising her because normal politeness had never been one of his attributes—except where the chairman was concerned and then it was nauseatingly excessive.

'Good morning, Chelsea. I've been waiting for you.'

The oil in his voice was thick enough to grease axles but she was beyond puzzling around what made the odious wretch tick and she put her briefcase down on her desk and decided that if he was waiting for her to apologise humbly for being late for the very first time ever then he would grow roots through the floorboards, and she said crisply, with just enough sarcasm to let him know exactly where he stood, 'About your proposition, Miles—nothing personal, of course, but you met my fiancé last night. Spends a lot of his time in the gym, keeping in shape.' Cool blue eyes denigrated his pampered portliness. 'Added to which, he's the jealous type. Know what I mean?'

Miles obviously did. He flushed to the roots of his thinning hair and his words came out in a rush, past a smile that was patently forced.

'I had no idea you were involved with anyone, let alone engaged to be married. Had I done so then obviously——' He broke off, in difficulties, then forced himself on, not looking at her, moving towards the door like a crab. 'I just wanted you to know that I'll be lunching with the chairman on Wednesday of next week. I'll put in a word on your behalf,' he promised, beginning to gabble. 'I can say without conceit that Sir Leonard takes my advice and opinions seriously. I don't take up my new position for another eight weeks, as you know, and I think I can safely say that, long before then,

I shall have persuaded him out of his prejudice against women in top managerial positions.'

He was halfway through the door and Chelsea could only guess at the effort behind his parting remark of, 'I'm sure you're open-minded enough to forget my mistake. Forgive and forget, eh, my dear? And I just know you'll make a first-rate head of department—with a directorship in the offing, if I know anything about it!'

She sat down heavily as soon as the door closed behind him, feeling for the edge of the chair with the back of her knees. She could hardly believe she had heard all that!

She had staked everything on Miles being a physical as well as a moral coward, guessing that if he could be made to believe she was about to be married to a man much younger and stronger than he—a hot-tempered, jealous man—then he would stop trying to blackmail her into going to bed with him.

That she had been prepared for. Prepared to see him back down, the loss of face that would have sent him on his spiteful way to Sir Leonard not coming into the equation because telling him, by implication, that she was deeply in love with another man, committed to him, would not have been so insulting, thereby putting her career in jeopardy, as if she had simply said, 'Thanks but no thanks. Go ahead and do your worst.'

She certainly hadn't expected to see him grovel, promising to make every effort on her behalf. It had come as a shock. She had resigned herself to having to make her own application to a chairman whose attitudes were firmly rooted in the Victorian age. She would have done her best and taken her chances, even though the outcome would have been—quite unfairly—uncertain.

It took her a full ten minutes to get over the success of her own wild scheme but, that accomplished, she got down to work with a will and didn't look up from the paperwork she was poring over until the secretary she shared with Miles came in with her coffee at eleven-thirty.

Molly was bursting to say something, and, as usual, came straight out with it.

'Where's your ring? Or is it too valuable to wear to work?' She stood with her arms akimbo, her cheerful grin very wide today. 'No wonder you never appeared to notice the way Jake Preston's been mooning over you these last six months. Bigger fish to fry—talk about a dark horse!'

'Sorry?' Chelsea had been engrossed in tricky financial costings and she looked up at Molly, her expression abstracted, and the secretary made an inelegant face.

'Don't come all enigmatic with me—the secret's well and truly out. Hang on.' She scuttled away and was back within moments, pushing a folded newspaper under Chelsea's nose. 'According to my old granny, you can't believe half you read in the papers. But deny that if you can!'

She could, of course she could, Chelsea acknowledged inwardly, her stomach performing a sudden somersault. Deny it and, as far as Miles's rage and spite were concerned, put her chances of promotion back about a thousand years.

The photograph of her, gazing up at an undeniably devastating Quinn, had caught a fleeting expression that made her look idiotically besotted. It was nauseating.

And the headline made her stomach feel as if it had taken off for outer space, leaving her well and truly behind.

'GEM-TYCOON PINNED DOWN AT LAST!'

And Molly said, 'I won't pretend I'm not green with envy—but I'll leave you to gloat in peace. Drink your coffee before it goes cold.'

Chelsea was too appalled to speak and sat staring at the newsprint long after Molly had walked from the room, her eyes incredulous. But she should have expected this. There had been enough reporters at the launch party last night, after all. Not one of them would have passed up on an item like this. And could Quinn, Quinn of the laid-back, easy charm, the lazy, seen-to-be-doing-nothing playboy, actually be the 'tycoon' of the legend? Or was that merely reporters' licence?

Dragging herself out of her daze of incredulity, she forced herself to concentrate on the accompanying paragraph, groaning softly as she read,

> Hitherto confirmed bachelor, Quinn Ryder, billionaire head of the internationally renowned Ryder-Gem empire, finally bowed to fate in the shape of the lovely Chelsea Viner when he proudly announced their engagement at the launch party of the new and exclusive Manhattan range of jewellery last night.

Groaning, she rested her head in her hands, her long fingers digging into her skull. How could she have trotted over to the legendary head of the Ryder-Gem empire and blithely asked him to pretend to be her fiancé? How could she? Just thinking about it made her feel ill. And what was almost worse, she had scathingly accused him of being a good-for-nothing, sponging layabout—or as good as!

She would never trust her own judgement again—based on outward appearances and gossip. Never!

The shrill of the phone came as a welcome distraction and she said quickly, 'Chelsea Viner, can I help you?', hoping to hear there was a crisis somewhere in the department, some sort of panic that would take her mind off the events of the past hours.

'You bet your sweet life you can!' There was no mistaking the smoky, slightly amused tones of Quinn Ryder and her insides began to cringe. He was the very last person she wanted to talk to right now; she needed to come to terms with the way she'd made such a fool of herself before she could face him, making the necessary apologies. 'But in the meantime I'm taking you to lunch,' he continued, unaffected by the silence coming from her end.

'I'm sorry,' she said through tight lips, not meaning it. This was something she could cope with. When turning down dates in the past her excuse of pressure of work had always worked well. And it would work this time because even though she did owe him an apology she wasn't ready to face making it yet. 'I really can't make the time. There's far too much on.'

As head of a huge international gemstone empire he would understand that business commitments came first, and maybe this evening, when she'd thought out precisely what to say to him, she could present herself at the door of the penthouse, make her contrition known and slip away. And that would be the end of the whole embarrassing business.

But Quinn said, 'I'm picking you up in half an hour. Be ready.' He sounded almost bored, as if her excuse was more tiresome than valid.

'It's out of the question,' she snipped straight back. He might not be the idle playboy of her earlier assumptions, but that didn't give him the right to act as though her work were of no importance. All thoughts of contrition had left her head but when his voice came acidly,

'I presume you've read the morning papers? Then you'll know we have a great deal to discuss,' it came flooding back with a vengeance. He would have to be one of the most eligible bachelors around; no wonder the announcement of his engagement had caused such a stir in the Press. And when he tacked on, 'Head office have been turning reporters away in droves all morning and I've had my mother and both my sisters tying up the telephone lines to my suite since breakfast,' she bit down hard on her lower lip and groaned.

He sounded coldly angry, and she could understand that. What had started out as a quiet deception, just a couple of words to warn Miles off, had ended up as a national news item. True, she hadn't known who he was at the time, or imagined that the lie would have gone any further, but he wouldn't be thinking that way. He would be thinking of the possible embarrassment to him and his family when the Press realised that a wedding would never take place.

'I repeat, be ready,' he bit out, and the line went dead, and Chelsea grimaced, pulling her lips back against her teeth, bowing—albeit ungraciously—to the inevitable.

* * *

He drove her out of town and they lunched at an exclusive restaurant overlooking the Thames, on a glass-sided terrace that caught the welcome breeze from the river.

'I'm sorry—for everything,' she'd said as soon as he'd handed her into the car outside her office block then tacked on, getting it over, 'I can't apologise enough. I shouldn't have—— '

And words failed her as he'd turned his head and given her a long, unreadable look, saying, 'So you should be.'

Her face went red. She stared ahead at the milling traffic and fumed. It hadn't been easy to take the blame for everything on her own shoulders and his acceptance of her apology could have been more gracious, so she reminded him tartly, 'If you'd behaved more circumspectly at that party instead of raising your voice and—and pawing me...' Her cheeks grew even more heated as she recalled precisely how it had felt to be held so closely against that powerful, whippy body, how his hands had roved so shamelessly. 'If you'd behaved like a normal man, instead of like a child let loose in a sweet shop, then no one would have cottoned on and we wouldn't be splashed all over the papers this morning!'

'You can't know much about men if you think my behaviour, given the circumstances, was abnormal.' He glanced at her briefly, his golden eyes wicked and she sagged back against the soft leather upholstery, her mouth a defeated pout.

He had an answer to everything, damn him! And he'd hit the nail on the head. She didn't know much about men. Except that every last one of them should have been christened Trouble at birth.

She stared hard at the road ahead but, despite herself, her eyes slid sideways and fastened on the long, slim masculine hands on the wheel. Her breath felt thick in her throat as she recalled how those hands had taken liberties with her body and she had to ask him to repeat himself when he told her, 'As it happens, I thought you were apologising for the way you accused me of wasting my talents and energies. I'm not too concerned about the hullabaloo in the Press. In fact, it couldn't have happened at a more convenient time.'

That was about the last thing she had expected to hear him say and Chelsea was about to take him up on that, but he didn't give her time, going on, 'You shouldn't categorise so readily. It's perfectly possible to work to the top of one's abilities and still make time to relax, have fun. Your trouble is, you don't know how to enjoy yourself.'

If he thought she had allowed herself to be forced into having lunch with him in order to listen to a lecture on her lifestyle, then he would have to be disabused. Not that it was any business of his, of course, but she asked him coolly, 'And what would you know about my ability to enjoy myself?'

'Observation. Close and interested observation over the past few weeks.' Again that wicked sideways glance, eyes lingering for one shattering second on the voluptuous pout of her lips, dropping with overt suggestion to the generous curve of her breasts, curves that not even the most severely styled jacket could disguise or magic away.

After that Chelsea had deemed it wiser to hold her tongue and now they were sitting in the sun, at a table overlooking the Thames. Quinn had done full justice to the delicious roulades of smoked salmon they'd chosen to start the meal, but Chelsea had only picked at hers, not knowing if she'd be able to eat any of the light salad she'd ordered to follow.

For something to do, she sipped the Pol Roger, which was as delicious as it was expensive. She wrinkled her nose appreciatively and sipped some more, enjoying the slide of the cold, crisp liquid against her throat. She was far too hot but had refused to part with her suit jacket, not wanting to have to cope with the inevitable way his sinful gaze would rest on her upper body, the lush curves blatantly obvious beneath the thin fabric of her blouse.

So far he'd kept up a light flow of conversation, mainly in the form of idly-put questions regarding her background. And as her background, such as it was, was nothing to do with him—or anyone else, for that matter—her end of the chit-chat had comprised the odd grunt or two punctuated by half a dozen throw-away shrugs. So he wouldn't be exactly bowled over by her sparkling company, but what of it?

She was a private person and he surely hadn't insisted on taking her to lunch in order to delve into her past. He must be saving the crunch until later.

That made her nervous; more nervous, rather. And she looked at the crisply innovative salad that had just been placed in front of her, at the thinly carved slices of meat and tried to hide a shudder.

Watching as he cut into his steak *au poivre*, she picked up her glass and drained it and recklessly jogged his memory.

'What did you mean when you said that the splash in the papers about our mythical engagement couldn't have come at a better time?' The remark had puzzled her because surely a man in his position would find it tiresome, to say the very least, to have to explain, not only to his family, but to the people he worked with, people at the top of the world-famous gem empire, why a wedding would never take place?

One black brow arched upwards very slightly but the smile he gave her was sheer unadulterated charm as he leaned forward to refill her wine glass, his voice a smoky purr as he told her, 'I've had a particularly persistent female on my back for months. If she—Sandy—thinks I'm madly in love and about to be married she'll finally get the message and move out of my life.'

Chelsea wished she hadn't asked. She hadn't thought he could be so cruel. And there was a tight knot of something nasty in her stomach—not jealousy, oh, most certainly not jealousy, but agonising distaste. The persistent Sandy must be one of the women Meryl had reported on. Was she one of the blondes, or the redhead?

She wished she wasn't here. Wished she hadn't swallowed two glasses of champagne in rapid succession. Wished she'd never met him.

But her moment of miserable silliness didn't last long and she soon dismissed it as being just that. She couldn't possibly be hurt because he was a self-confessed louse. No, of course not. He had simply reinforced her firmly held convictions that emotional involvements were a waste of time, that love was a pretty word for lust, and that relationships between the sexes lasted precisely as long as the partners remained physically attractive to each other.

Pulling herself together, she forced herself to eat a curl of crunchy celery and, her slanting eyes commendably cool, managed to achieve the right inflexion of cynicism.

'Maybe Sandy—was that her name?—will do no such thing. She might be content to continue as your mistress, whether you're married or not. That's par for the course in your financially exalted circles, isn't it?'

Men like Quinn Ryder had the edge over the run-of-the-mill nine-to-fivers. They could afford to buy the women they fancied. Chelsea knew all about that, to her cost. And the hard, underbrow look he shot her didn't make her regret her tart opinion and she merely shrugged when he told her brusquely, 'In my experience women only want one thing. A plain gold band on the wedding finger as a passport to financial security for life. Not forgetting, of course, the opportunity to crow over the others who haven't been successful in bringing their matrimonial plans to fruition.'

'You're a cynic.' She cut into a wafer-thin slice of cold roast beef and he countered amusedly,

'So, my dear, are you.' He leaned back in his chair, watching from narrowed golden eyes as she ate, a tiny smile indenting the corners of his sensual mouth. 'In fact, I'm beginning to think we have a great deal in common.' His smile deepened and there was a devil looking out of those black-fringed golden eyes now. 'Once I teach you how to unwind and play, we're going to get along like the clichéd house on fire.'

The implication being that she should play with him. And one look into his eyes was enough to tell her that he didn't have squash or Scrabble in mind! She looked away quickly. Did he think she was a fool? Or easily bought, like others of his female acquaintanceship maybe?

The beginnings of anger stirred deep inside her, but she ousted it firmly. Might as well get angry with a cat for catching a mouse. Quinn Ryder was by nature a predator, the female of the species his prey. And the way he conducted his life was no business of hers. Stupid to allow herself to feel anything where he was concerned— even anger.

'Thanks for the offer,' she riposted drily, 'but I have neither the time nor the inclination.'

No comment, merely the amused twitch of a highly sensual male mouth. Chelsea laid her cutlery down. She had eaten as much as she could manage, her lunch break was over, they were miles away from her office and he still hadn't told her why this meeting had been necessary.

Time to find out, even if she didn't like the answer, and something told her that, whatever it was, it would be unpredictable—like the man himself.

The only possible reason he could have had for wanting to talk with her had to be the Press announcements, so she looked him straight in the eye and demanded, 'How long are we going to let the phoney engagement ride?'

He relaxed even further on his chair, one arm negligently hooked over the back, a pussy-cat smile on his unforgettable face as he enquired, 'Coffee?'

'No! Thank you.' She remembered her manners, just in time and tried to stop fuming. How any man, this laid-back, could control a business empire was simply beyond her!

But before she had time to restate her tart question he told her easily, 'Just as long as it takes. You haven't got a lover who might take umbrage—otherwise you would have got him to take the part you assigned to me regarding Robartes's blackmail attempts. And I want to rid myself of a clinging female, once and for all. So that leaves us where?' He paused before shooting her a level look and answering his own question. 'Sitting pretty. Safe within the walls of our own charade for the time being. You get Robartes off your back—before you arrived at the party last night, begging me for favours, he was blatantly doing his best to sell Triple A. Got some idea in his head to do with Ryder-Gem disbanding its own advertising department. So as long as he thinks we're a permanent and serious item he's not going to come sniffing around you, is he?'

Chelsea didn't answer. She couldn't. Quinn's turn of phrase had made her feel ill. But he was right, of course, and she would tell him so, just as soon as she got her stomach back under control. But she didn't get the chance because his next words took the breath out of her lungs.

'So, for starters, we'll go visit my mother. Take a couple of weeks.' And, at her pole-axed gasp, 'That will reinforce the announcement and look absolutely natural. I've already cleared it with your superiors at Triple A. As from this evening you have two weeks' leave. We'll drive up to Monk's Norton on Sunday morning. Mother is expecting us.'

CHAPTER FOUR

QUINN was joking, of course he was. Or out of his mind. Cool blue eyes lifted to engage the dancing golden lights of his across the debris of their meal and Chelsea made her voice light but firm, as if she were speaking to a mischievous child.

'Try to be serious. I'm perfectly willing to say nothing to contradict the engagement fiction. But contact me before you decide to end the charade, so that we can dovetail our stories.'

She flicked an imaginary crumb from the lapel of her jacket, pleased with the way she had handled that. Visit his mother, indeed! Then froze with something approaching real horror as he informed her blandly, 'I'm completely serious. Your leave has been arranged, Mother is expecting us, and we will leave for Monk's Norton on Sunday morning.' He signed a cheque with a heavy gold pen and handed it over to a hovering waiter and Chelsea shot to her feet.

Her whole body was rigid with outrage. She stamped towards the exit and when he fell in step beside her she whispered fiercely out of the corner of her mouth, 'How dare you? I have no intention of going anywhere with you, let alone to visit your mother!' To her aggravation, she stumbled over a step and angrily shrugged off the hand he had instinctively used to steady her. 'You had no right to interfere at my place of work—no right at all. I take my leave when it suits me and, at the moment, it doesn't.'

'Apparently, it rarely does. Suit you, I mean,' Quinn uttered drily. 'You never take your full holiday entitlement, so I was told. In my opinion, you've made refusing to relax into an art-form.'

And spending two weeks in his company would relax her? Huh! Chelsea snorted inelegantly and Quinn looked down at her hot, cross face, a flicker of a smile crossing his memorable features. He had opened the car door and was waiting for her to get in, his big body between her and a bus-stop she'd glimpsed way down the road.

It would take her hours to get back to central London by bus. Besides, she didn't have any cash with her. Escape was impossible. Sighing, she flounced into the passenger-seat, resigning herself to endure his company on the drive back. Arrogant swine! Telling her what to do, interfering with her work schedule. Well, he wasn't getting away with it. No power on earth would make her meekly comply with his dictates!

Staring straight ahead, her arms crossed high across her chest, Chelsea waited until he'd pulled the car off the car park and on to the road and then attacked witheringly, 'What kind of man would lie to his own mother? Say he was about to be married, when he wasn't? What do you——'

'She knows it's a sham,' he cut in smoothly. 'I explained everything. I also put my sisters in the picture when they phoned this morning. So everyone who matters knows the truth.' Briefly, he gave her an intense look. 'So you won't have to pretend to anyone, will you?

That way, you won't get any misguided ideas about the permanency of our engagement, or the outcome of it.'

Insolent bastard! Warning her off, was he? Chelsea dragged in a deep breath. No point in losing her temper. She told him with cool acid, 'Don't fret. You're perfectly safe. I have no intention of marrying. Ever. And even if I did you would come way down the bottom of the list.'

She allowed him to digest that interesting snippet of information in silence, keeping her mouth firmly closed. No point in spending the remainder of the journey lobbing insults around. She could think of nothing more demeaning and unproductive. And she couldn't imagine why she, who very rarely lost her temper, letting emotions get out of control, had allowed this one man to flick her on the raw so often.

Besides, she was keeping the best bit until last. And when he pulled up outside her office block she undid her seatbelt and firmly informed him, 'I am now going to cancel my leave. Please give my apologies to your mother and explain that I found it impossible to drop everything at such short notice.'

He couldn't physically force her to go with him, and it was high time he learned that simply because he had looks and charm, great wealth and an undoubted social position he couldn't get his own way all the time.

She gave him a tilt-headed glance, a glance that said, 'Let's see how you get out of that, Mister. The ball's in your court.' And he returned her gaze steadily, taking up the unspoken challenge.

'As you please. However, I feel I should warn you— should you be so misguided as to cancel my arrangements, I shall have no compunction in going to Robartes and informing him that the whole engagement announcement had been your idea, that there isn't an atom of truth in it, that it was nothing but a sick joke, at his expense, designed to make him look a fool. And then you could kiss your promotion hopes goodbye for good, couldn't you?'

Chelsea went cold all over as she lifted wide, incredulous eyes to his. The relaxed, charming mask she had grown so used to had been suddenly ripped from his features, making his face hard, almost brutal. She was, she recognised bleakly, seeing the real Quinn Ryder, a man who would stop at nothing to get what he wanted. When and how he wanted it.

In the event, Chelsea was more relieved than anything when Quinn called for her at nine on Sunday morning, the time he had said they'd be leaving for Monk's Norton, in Shropshire, where, apparently, his mother lived. She had spent all Friday evening and the whole of Saturday curled up in her small sitting-room, the phone unplugged to evade the importunings of the Press, magazine editors and the like.

If she hadn't known it before, she did now—the head of the Ryder-Gem empire had a name that rang bells. She would be heartily thankful to be out of range of reporters who wanted to know how it felt to be the future bride of the wealthiest, most eligible bachelor around.

'Don't look round,' Quinn ordered as he marched her through the underground car park, one hand gripping her elbow, the other occupied with her luggage.

And she whispered hoarsely, 'Do you think they're waiting? Will they follow us?'

He bit out tersely, 'Anyone who tries will find their teeth where they shouldn't be.'

She believed him, and he hadn't needed to ask what she was talking about so he must have been pestered, too, and it obviously went against the grain and she wondered why he had allowed himself to be drawn into this charade in the first place; why, having agreed to the pretence, he hadn't kept his voice down at that party, his hands to himself. Why he had almost gone out of his way to ensure that everyone there was aware of the so-called engagement.

Unless he had a brain that worked at the speed of light, she reasoned as he settled her into the front of the BMW and strode around to the driver's side. He had admitted that he wanted to keep up the pretence for a while, a fool-proof way to get rid of a clinging female. So when she'd bounced up, all bright-eyed and bushy-tailed, asking him to pretend to be her fiancé, just for a couple of minutes, his laser-like brain must have conceived it as the ideal way of getting rid of the unwanted Sandy. The inconvenience of having hordes of gossip columnists panting at his heels something he could cope with.

And that was borne out when, as they pulled on to the quiet Sunday morning streets, she heaved a sigh of relief and told him, 'I expected to see a whole troupe of reporters, notebooks at the ready, camped out on the street.'

'I had my Press-officer give out that we had chartered a private jet last night. Were bound for a hideaway in the Bahamas to enjoy a little pre-nuptial privacy. So don't be alarmed if you read that you and I are sunning ourselves, *au naturel*, on a sun-kissed beach on the other side of the world.' As they halted at traffic-lights he gave her the benefit of a lightly caressing, amused glance. 'At least it will get them off our backs for a while and no one but family knows about the house at Monk's Norton.'

The traffic-lights changed and the car shot forward and Chelsea turned an uncomfortable pink. He might have fooled the reporters, and he might be used to letting the whole world know that he and his current lady were enjoying the privacy of a paradisal island retreat, but her reputation would be in tatters, particularly when news of a 'break-up' hit the gossip columns.

But what did her reputation matter since the majority of her colleagues at work took it for granted that couples slept together, a wedding in the offing or not? She hadn't heard from her father in years and her mother—well, who knew where she was? She had walked out, washing her hands of both her daughters, five years ago. So that left her sister, and Joannie was abroad, getting over a messy divorce; she probably wouldn't notice lurid items about her, Chelsea, if they jumped out of the newsprint and bit her.

However, she did have her job, and promotion to look forward to. She understood now why Miles had been so eager to put her name forward. You scratch my back and I'll scratch yours. I'll make sure you get the promotion you want and you can have a word in your fiancé's ear and persuade him to give the Ryder-Gem account to Triple A when he disbands his own advertising department. A scoop as big as that would put him even more firmly in his chairman's good books!

Little did Miles realise that Quinn would take about as much notice of any wheedlings coming from her direction as he would take of a fly buzzing around someone else's ears! She heaved a terrible sigh and Quinn said, 'Cheer up! We'll stop for coffee in about half an hour and I'll fill you in on Monk's Norton—the village and the house. I promise you, you won't regret the time you spend there.'

By the time they'd had coffee and were on their way again Chelsea was beginning to relax. Quinn was undeniably good company, a charming, attentive companion, his conversation both intelligent and humorous. And if it weren't for the way, over the leisurely coffee break they'd taken, his eyes had made several attentive assessments of her face and form, she would have admitted to enjoying herself immensely.

He probably couldn't help himself, she excused, slipping a tape into the deck. He was an out-and-out womaniser and 'sizing up the talent' would come naturally to him. When he got to know her better he would soon realise that she was immune to flirtatious males. All males, in fact. Besides, she comforted herself, his mother would be around to help keep him in his place! His sisters, too.

'Shall I get to meet your sisters?' She voiced her thoughts over the muted Vivaldi. 'Do they live at home with your mother?'

'Erica—she's around your age—lives in Norfolk. Happily married and heavily pregnant for the second time,' he imparted, his attention on the road ahead as he left the motorway. 'And Cassie, just twenty-one and the baby of the family, is at a London drama school. She shares an outrageous bed-sit with an even more outrageous girlfriend—a fellow student. She's fun, I think you'd like her. Erica's more staid; she tries to mother everyone in sight. I think she was born old. Come to think of it,' he grinned, his concentration still firmly on the road, 'you might find you have more in common with her.'

Which Chelsea didn't take as a compliment. She didn't try to mother all and sundry but 'staid', 'born old'? Was that the way he saw her? And if he did, did it matter?

She turned her head, giving up on that line of conversation. Inexplicably, tears stung the back of her eyes and she blinked them away. Nothing to do with his unflattering opinion of her, of course. Nothing. Simply the strain of the last few days.

Thankfully, he seemed to have decided to think his own thoughts, and the countryside they were passing through now was beautiful enough to take her mind off her troubles.

She had been unprepared for the midsummer delights of rural Shropshire. City girls born and bred, she and Joannie had been taken to the coast from time to time for family holidays that had invariably turned out to be domestic disasters. Nothing, it had seemed, could prevent their parents from bickering.

Now the leafy stillness of the lanes enchanted her, small villages with old stone churches spiring above them, cottage gardens ablaze with tangled colour. Everywhere looked drowsy, as if the land and its inhabitants were still waiting for the twentieth century to come along.

Chelsea wound down the window at her side and ec-statically breathed in the hay-scented air, and Quinn said, 'Not long now. We turn off here,' and swung the car between two stone pillars on to a track that seemed to lead into the heart of a wood. A great cathedral-like wood, the giant columns of the beech trunks dappled gold and green where the sunlight filtered down through the overhead canopy of fresh early summer leaves.

On and on for about a mile until the woods eventually admitted a smooth, grassy clearing on either side of the track. And ahead of them stood the house, a gem of Tudor architecture created in ancient grey stone with gabled roofs and tall Elizabethan chimneys.

'This is fantastic,' Chelsea breathed, her wide eyes taking in everything from the house itself to the layout of low, formal box hedges enclosing parterres of brilliant flowers which lay to the front and sides of the house itself, and the glimpse, beyond, through a wide stone archway, of solid outbuildings, garages and a stable-block, she supposed. 'I don't think I've ever seen anything so lovely.'

'I'm glad you approve. As I said, I don't think you'll find your stay here a hardship,' Quinn told her lightly as he halted the car in front of the steps that led up to the main porch. He took his hands from the wheel and leaned back, slightly angled against the door, one arm resting along the back of her seat. 'And I'm going to enjoy teaching you how to relax. It's something I've been wanting to do for weeks, since I first saw you.'

His eyes were wicked, the smile that curved along the line of his beautifully crafted mouth taking on an impudence that shocked her as he allowed the downward drift of his gaze to linger on her body.

The loose turquoise top and snug-fitting white jeans she had chosen to travel in offered no protection at all from the erotic onslaught, she thought distractedly, feeling her skin grow heated, every nerve-end tingling wherever those devilish eyes touched.

A silky strand of midnight hair had somehow escaped the strict confines of her chignon and he lazily lifted his hand from the back of her seat and ran the softly perfumed length through his fingers and the atmosphere inside the car suddenly came alive, vibrant, pulsing with strange unspoken, unthinkable yearnings. And when the backs of his fingers brushed languorously against her earlobe, scalding her with impossible sensation, Chelsea gave a silent, inner scream of repudiation.

Then gritted her teeth, holding her body rigid, holding back the words that would tell him to stop taking liberties, stop touching. She instinctively knew that such a wildness would let him know how much his slightest and patently meaningless touch affected her. Violent protestations would only serve to alert him to his surely as yet unsuspected power. Better to play cool, let him think his touch did nothing, couldn't reach her.

Calm down, she instructed her hammering pulses, then saw her salvation in the shape of a furiously pedalling cyclist and said, in a voice that came out on a shamefully febrile croak, 'Someone's coming.'

'Going.' Quinn's hand stopped making havoc, allowing Chelsea's temperature to drop back towards normal. He tooted the horn and the cyclist, a wiry woman in or around the mid-thirties mark, paused, lifted a waving hand, wobbled precariously and then resumed her pedalling, spinning down the track. Before the woman had disappeared between the flanking trees Chelsea had got herself back together, was out of the car, standing in the warm sunshine, waiting for Quinn to emerge.

'Mrs Cranforth, from the village,' Quinn explained, pocketing the car keys, drawing Chelsea's unwilling attention to the sexy fit of his lightweight cream trousers. He walked round the car towards her and she stoically ignored the sudden and unwelcome electrical jolt in the region of her stomach and tried to look immensely interested as he carried on, 'Now that her children are all at school she comes in to help out. Cooking, cleaning and so on. Nine-thirty until four, not at all on Saturdays, and until midday on Sundays to help prepare lunch.' He draped an arm around her shoulders, making her flinch beneath the physical contact. 'When I'm not here she merely comes in to flick a duster around and make endless pots of tea for old Jerry Meakes who looks after the gardens.'

Which meant that his mother would be the homely type, happy to do her own cooking when she was home on her own, and that was nice. Her own mother, when she had bothered at all, had opened tins.

'Hello, you two!' The clear, bell-like voice brought Chelsea's attention to the main door, now open beneath the sheltering porch, which was carved from silvery oak, and she immediately revised her assumption. If this small, elegant creature, her silvering hair drawn back in a smooth French pleat, her make-up subdued yet perfect, was Quinn's mother then images of gingham aprons,

ample bosoms and home-made steak and kidney pud-
dings had to be laughably off-mark.

'Quinn, darling—I expected you an hour ago.' The
tiny woman's intelligent yellow eyes rested briefly on her
son's hand as it lay on Chelsea's shoulder and Chelsea
felt her face go red. It was as if the other woman was
perfectly well aware of the shuddery sensations that were
being transmitted from that strong masculine hand, and
vaguely pitied her.

Sons couldn't hide anything from their mothers; Mrs
Ryder would be well aware of the way Quinn used
women, used them and tossed them aside when passion
was spent and boredom set in.

The very thought of being pitied appalled her and her
chin came up in an unconsciously defiant gesture. She
wasn't Quinn's woman, and never would be, and Quinn
said, 'We stopped for coffee and took an inordinate
amount of time over it. The company was too delightful
to give me any urge to rush.' His hand dropped from
her shoulder to the small of her back, gentling her
forward, and Chelsea could have hit him. Mrs Ryder
knew there was no truth in the engagement story but the
words he said, the very timbre of his voice, would give
her the impression that they were very much more than
simply neighbours in an apartment block!

He had placed himself directly behind her now, both
hands on her shoulders, his body so close that it scorched
her spine. It was as if he were blocking her escape route
and was, as ever, dominating her, manoeuvring her for
his own slightly suspect ends. And his voice was as soft
as melted honey, embarrassing her still further.

'Ma, meet Chelsea Viner. I've told you all about her and I want you to be great friends. Get acquainted while I bring in the luggage.'

The momentary intimate extra pressure of his hands on her shoulders, his fingertips transmitting a message directly from his body to hers, was something Chelsea could well have done without. But then he was gone, loping back to the car, and his mother said, 'Call me Elaine, and do come through. I'm sure you could do with something long and cold after the excitement of the last few days.'

She would have gone to hell with the devil himself to escape Quinn's more than disturbing presence, which was pretty wimpish of her, Chelsea conceded irritably, falling in step beside the exquisitely *soignée* Elaine as they entered the main hall together.

She could deal with flirtatious males, even those with openly lustful intent, with one hand tied behind her back, metaphorically speaking, so why throw a wobbly whenever Quinn decided to turn the megawatt power of his charm on her? He was no different from any other of the male species.

She ignored the wicked little voice inside her head that insisted he was, he very much was, and threw herself into admiring what she could see of his mother's home. Not that she actually had to try because the main hallway was magnificent.

Clearly used as a living-room, it ran almost the length of the house and boasted a carved staircase that soared gracefully up to the gallery above. And warm summer sunlight streamed in through the mullioned windows, lying in pools of gold on the dark oak floor, splashing against the panelled walls.

'This is perfect,' Chelsea said, and meant it. It beat her ultra-modern flat—expensive though it was—into a cocked hat and left the tall, narrow house in Stepney, where she had been brought up, standing.

And Elaine said softly,

'When Quinn first found it he fell in love at first sight. But that's him all over—he doesn't give his heart lightly, but when he does it's given for keeps.'

'That's nice,' Chelsea approved. There was something about the lovely old house that was having a calming effect on her, giving her a sense of tranquillity she hadn't experienced since Miles Robartes had tried to blackmail her into his bed. She could afford, for once, to be magnanimous. 'You're lucky to have a son prepared to go to enough trouble to find you the perfect place to live.'

'Oh, but I don't live here, at least, not permanently.' Elaine sounded lightly amused. She was standing behind one of the squashy, chintz-upholstered armchairs which were grouped around the cavernous ingle fireplace, decorated now with a huge earthenware bowl filled with spikes of pale blue delphiniums. 'Sit down while I fix that long, cold drink I promised. No——' She moved away as Chelsea did as she was told, sinking into the blissfully comfortable chair, her feet on one of the fine old rugs which were scattered around. 'No, this is Quinn's home. After his father died, when Quinn took over the business, he lived out of suitcases and never seemed to stop travelling from one company office to the other. But three years ago he decided to make roots and found this place—after a fairly exhaustive search, I may say.'

She handed Chelsea a tall glass, the colourless sparkly liquid laced with ice and lemon slices, then took a chair opposite, crossing elegant legs clad in sheer black silk.

'I have an apartment in Paris, but I come here from time to time. Quinn thinks it's because I want to keep an eye on him——' her yellow eyes crinkled with a warmth Chelsea found instantly appealing '—but actually it's because I'm beginning to feel my age. When the hectic social life I lead in Paris begins to tell, I use this place to recharge my batteries, rusticate and frankly enjoy it.' She took a delicate sip from her own glass, her eyes sparkling over the rim. 'I don't tell him the truth, though. I do have an image to preserve. If he thought his poor old mum was ready to be pensioned off, he'd be more impossible than ever. When one has a son as self-assured and forceful as Quinn, one has to keep one's end up, by any means!'

'I can imagine!' Chelsea grinned, taking another cool swallow of her vodka and tonic. With a man like Quinn it would be difficult, if not impossible, to keep the upper hand.

'Now tell me exactly what led up to that astonishing engagement announcement,' Elaine prompted, settling back in her chair, her smile pure mischief, leaving Chelsea in no doubt about where Quinn had inherited all his devastating charm from. 'He told me it was nothing more than an expedient sham but, man-like, glossed over the details as being irrelevant. So do tell all!'

So Chelsea told her how it had all started, and what had happened next, noting that Elaine's fine eyebrows lifted to her hairline when Sandy's name was mentioned. Perhaps Quinn had managed to keep the lovelorn clinger secret from his intelligent, sophisticated parent.

Elaine got up and took Chelsea's glass for a refill and when she pressed the ice-cold glass back into the younger woman's hand there was a definite edge of amusement around her careless, 'And Quinn decided to whisk you down here, away from it all. He's never brought a woman here before. He tells me this place is sacrosanct. The only person, apart from family, who knows of its existence is the most senior of his PAs—and he only knows the phone number, to be used solely in a case of catastrophic emergency.'

'It was the Press,' Chelsea answered sagely—the unaccustomed intake of spirits before lunch slowing down her thought processes but making her feel very wise at the same time. 'He had to get me away, suppose he thought I might give way under the pressure and admit it was a hoax. And then where would he be with poor Sandy?' She wrinkled her brow. But Quinn had already put the Press off the scent, hadn't he? At least, his Press officer had.

And Elaine responded drily, 'Don't waste your sympathies on her. And I would have thought that son of mine had enough common sense to realise that you, of all people, wouldn't spill the beans, unless you actually wanted that nasty little man—Robartes?—to take his revenge. Ah, there you are, darling. Join us in a drink?'

Quinn had been in and out, carrying luggage up the stairs, and Chelsea had deliberately ignored him. Talking to Elaine was easy, she was growing to like her more and more, but when he sat on the arm of his mother's chair and gave her the benefit of his devastating smile she found herself smiling back unrestrainedly and had to give herself a mental shove when he said, 'Not for me, Ma. I'll show Chelsea to her room; she probably wants to freshen up before lunch.' He moved lazily to his feet and held out a hand to her, but she ignored it; of course she did. She wasn't fool enough to take it. Oh, no.

'Then I'll see you both in a little while.' Elaine picked up a magazine from a side-table. 'No hurry. Lunch is cold so nothing will spoil.'

Chelsea had no option but to follow Quinn, up the magnificent staircase and on to the gallery. It was panelled, like the hall, doors opening off it, and their feet sank into the thick luxury of carpets that had the look and feel of the priceless.

'I've given you the end room, next to mine,' he told her, opening a door and waiting for her to precede him. The glimpse of the room, seen through the partly opened door, told her it was beautiful and everything was an unsolvable enigma. And instead of moving she tipped her head, looking up at him, a puzzled frown shadowing her eyes to purple.

Why had he insisted on her coming here? They were comparative strangers, after all. Monk's Norton was sacrosanct, so Elaine had said, not even his business colleagues knew of its existence, never mind his women. And he'd dealt with the problem of the Press, so...

The eyes that were holding hers were hot, darker than she remembered them being before, and as they drifted slowly down to her lips his own mouth softened and she knew.

It was time she stopped kidding herself. She knew why she was here. He was sexually interested. She'd sensed that even before she'd asked him to take part in the engagement charade. Sensed it, but refused to admit it, putting his flirtatious manner down to mere habit. Ignoring the verbal and physical messages because she hadn't wanted to know. To admit to knowing exactly what he'd been telling her would have meant she would have had to face up to it.

And she was facing up to it now, and it made her very nervous. And then, as if her tiny involuntary gasp were a signal he was programmed to pick up, he drew her with him through the door and closed it, turning her so that she was trapped between him and it. All too suddenly, all too much for her slightly fuddled mind to grasp, his body was against hers, not too close, but touching, touching from breast to thigh, making her breathless, seared by the male warmth of him, breathless, giddy and confused.

And then his mouth touched hers, taking her senses by storm. Lightly it touched, his lips moving gently, persuasively, tenderly stroking, making no demands, not yet. The feather-light kisses were igniting fires in her brain and she felt her breath come shallow and fast. She felt dizzy and hollow, at the same time strangely heavy, and, almost as if he had given instructions, her mouth opened beneath his.

Just for a moment he went still before, with a husky groan, he put the sensual onslaught into second gear, tasting her now, holding her closer, crushing her breasts against his heavy heartbeat, and her arms went around him with no effort at all, not thinking, her mind totally occupied with the flares of sheet-fire sensation that were threatening to send her out of her mind.

Chelsea had never, ever felt like this before. Not even when she'd believed herself in love with Roger had she experienced such... such sensations, felt so completely swamped by them. She didn't know what in the name of heaven was happening to her. She met the honeyed sweetness of his tongue with hers. And, what was more, she didn't care...

Quinn lifted his head and she gave a mew of protest, her hands objecting as he lifted them away from around his neck, and when she could focus her eyes again she saw that his own were alight with amused satisfaction, his lips curving, slow and sweet, as he told her huskily, 'We'd better call a halt for the time being. Otherwise Ma will deduce that we've found a way of satisfying our appetites that has nothing to do with her cold lunch.' He ran a finger over her parted, swollen lips. 'I'll see you downstairs in ten minutes.'

And she was too shocked to sense what was coming, to evade the sudden dip of his head, the careless parting brush of his lips on hers before he swung her stupefied body away from the door and let himself out, closing it firmly behind him.

CHAPTER FIVE

'TEN minutes,' Quinn had said, and ten minutes later Chelsea walked down the stairs, still incensed.

To have skulked in her room, fuming, while the afternoon ticked by would only have alerted him to the mental havoc he had wreaked, and she could do without that, couldn't she just!

His ego was already impossibly inflated, he thought he was God's gift—and then some. So give him an inkling of the mental turmoil he had created when he'd kissed her, and he would move in for the kill.

He needn't know a thing about the other part of it, the physical havoc. Thankfully, he was in no position to begin to guess at the way he had made her feel. So if she could shrug the whole episode off as just one of those things she would be in a much stronger defensive position if he tried anything on again.

She shouldn't have agreed to come here, she berated herself as she marched down the stairs, hastily fixing a smile on her face as Elaine came to meet her. Thank heavens for his mother, she thought, desperately trying to look and act like a normal house-guest as that lady said, 'We're eating in the breakfast-room; it's much cosier than the main dining-room, nearer the kitchen, too.' She tucked her arm companionably through Chelsea's, leading her towards the far end of the hall.

'We must ask Quinn to show you over the house this afternoon, let you get your bearings.'

No, thanks, Chelsea said inside her head. He would make a bee-line for the bedrooms. Then suggested with a laugh that was meant to be light but came out sounding strangled, 'Men are hopeless at that sort of thing. Why don't you show me round, when you have time?' Which earned her an assessing look which she tried to turn by showing an excessive interest in a series of small water-colours on the panelled walls, while not taking in the subject matter of any one of them.

Quinn was already in the breakfast-room, opening a bottle of white wine, and Chelsea felt her face go hot. Just remembering the way she'd allowed him to kiss her, had kissed him back, was going to give her nightmares for months.

Refusing wine—that vodka was responsible for her mindless submission to Quinn's kisses; it had to be, hadn't it?—she made a half-hearted attempt to eat, un-aware of her surroundings or of what was on her plate. Only aware of him, of his large presence opposite her at the circular table, of the way he watched from slightly hooded, lazy eyes, of the indefinable smile that lurked around the corners of his mouth. Of the way he was gloating!

She did her best to join in the general conversation, suspecting that her comments were, at best, inane, probably downright stupid, and leapt to her feet with unseemly haste when Elaine announced, 'We'll have coffee in the hall, shall we? Go on through—while I fetch it.'

'Let me help.' It was a cry from the heart, did they but know it. She wouldn't spend another second alone with Quinn if she could help it. And found herself pinned between Elaine's amused, intelligent glance and Quinn's,

'Ma's quite capable of carrying a coffee-pot on her own.' He then reinforced his accurate comment by reaching out to take her wrist in an inescapable grasp.

The touch of his fingers was like a brand and as soon as Elaine had left the room Chelsea wrenched her hand away, angrily rubbing the reddened skin, facing him, storm-clouds gathering in her slanting blue eyes.

'Don't touch me!'

'You sound like a melodramatic Victorian heroine.' His grin was infuriating. Nothing could faze him, shake his incredible cool. Except, she remembered, when he thought he couldn't get his own way. She'd seen the other side of his forceful character when she'd started out by flatly refusing to come down here. She didn't know which side of him frightened her the most.

But she wasn't going to let him know he could make her feel as confused and wary as a disorientated cat and when he said softly, 'You didn't object to being touched an hour ago,' she retorted with commendable cool,

'You took me by surprise.' Which was perfectly true. 'Think nothing more of the aberration, I certainly shan't.' Which wasn't true at all.

She stalked away then, her spine rigid. Philandering swine! No doubt he believed that every woman he took a passing fancy to was his for the taking. Well, he was going to discover that this one wasn't! He would have to back off, suffer a blow to his over-large ego from which, she hoped, he would take a long time to recover, when he learned he'd met his match in the cool, un-emotional Chelsea Viner.

That she had been neither cool nor unemotional ever since she'd begged him to agree to that pretence was something she didn't want to consider. And she flounced into the armchair she'd used earlier, snatched up the magazine Elaine had been reading and didn't look up until she heard the rattle of coffee-cups.

'No Quinn?' Elaine asked as Chelsea's stony face emerged from its hiding-place.

Chelsea shook her head, smiling a little, shaking her head, and watched as the monster's mother dealt deftly and neatly with the exquisite china, pouring coffee from a chased silver pot.

'Then it's just the two of us.' Elaine passed the cream-jug. 'Help yourself to sugar.' Her head tipped to one side consideringly. 'You two haven't had a spat, have you?'

'Good heavens, no!' Chelsea lied, wondering what his mother would say if she told her that as soon as they'd reached her bedroom he had tried to seduce her. Then felt the beginnings of a blush as she recalled how it had been Quinn himself who had called a halt, that her own treacherous body would probably have willingly gone wherever he had chosen to lead it! Covering her hot embarrassment as best she could, she tacked on quickly, 'We don't know each other well enough to quarrel,' compounding the lie because she had done nothing but fight with him, over one thing or another, ever since the night of the Ryder-Gem party.

Thankfully, Elaine didn't pursue the subject, talking of the garden instead. And Chelsea was only too pleased to take her up on her offer to show her around the grounds and happily followed her hostess out into the sunlight, hoping that a slow, peaceful amble would enable her to put the whole rather shaming episode in her bedroom into its proper perspective.

But she wasn't given the opportunity. As soon as they had passed through the cobbled courtyard to the rear of the lovely old house Chelsea felt her breath ripped away from her lungs, making speech, any kind of comment impossible.

'It is a surprise, isn't it?' Elaine smiled understandingly. 'It affects everyone this way at first.'

In a way it was like being on the deck of a huge ocean-going liner, Chelsea thought delightedly. For beyond the smoothly mown semi-circle of brilliant green grass the land dropped away precipitously and from there, as far as the eye could see in all directions, lay forest land, the tops of the trees, beneath eye-level, swaying idly in the summer breeze like gently rolling waves at sea, on and on to the blue horizon.

'There are paths going down the rock-face,' Elaine told her. 'Down to little valleys, streams, pools for swimming—the odd open glade or two, although you wouldn't think it from up here.'

'A descent that's definitely not to be undertaken solo.' A steely strand of warning ran through the softly spoken words, and Elaine turned, her face smiling,

'Quinn—we thought we'd lost you,' Elaine said, and Chelsea thought, I wish to heaven we had. Permanently. Because until he'd crept up behind them she'd been beginning to feel relaxed and now she was as strung up as piano wire again. And Elaine continued, tucking her arm through her son's, 'I was telling Chelsea about the pools in the forest, the glades where the bluebells grow—only they will be over now, of course. Or will they?'

'I know. I heard you.' He ignored her question about the bluebells and Chelsea didn't have to turn her head to know that he was looking directly at her. She could feel the wicked caress of those eyes. It was as if she had suddenly developed an extra sense. She refused to meet his eyes, knowing full well that she would meet a taunting reminder of what had happened earlier in those glittering, devilish golden depths.

Keeping her attention on the swaying tops of the forest trees, wishing she was down there among them, out of sight, away from him, wishing she'd never come here in the first place, she heard him say, 'If Chelsea wants a swim, Ma—and that's not such a bad idea at that—there's a perfectly good swimming-pool on the south courtyard, as you very well know. Far safer than tempting her to climb down a precipice. What were you trying to do? Get rid of her?'

It was said in a gently teasing tone, leaving Chelsea in no doubt how fond he was of his parent, and an unwilling smile hovered at the corners of her mouth as Elaine put in indignantly, 'Of course I wasn't! How could you even suggest such a thing? I was simply boasting about the delights of your property.'

And Chelsea thought, So he owns this lot, does he? No wonder he thinks he's omnipotent! And heard Elaine say,

'Yes, why don't you two take a swim and cool off while I catch up with some letters that should have been written weeks ago?'

Getting out of that one was easy. Chelsea turned then, her smile for Elaine.

'I didn't bring a swimsuit, so I'll have to pass on that.' Her metabolism wouldn't be able to cope with the sight of Quinn stripped down to swimming briefs, and the lord only knew what liberties he'd take if they got together in a secluded pool. But her relief at knowing that the occasion wouldn't arise was shattered when his mouth curved in a tigerish smile.

'I'm sure there'll be something among Cassie's things that Chelsea could use.'

And Elaine assented brightly, 'Now why didn't I think of that?' She explained to Chelsea, 'Wherever my youngest goes, she seems to leave half her wardrobe behind—and then complains she has nothing to wear! I'll have a root through the stuff she left behind the last time she stayed here. If there's a swimsuit among the clutter I'll drop it into your room.'

'Fine. Thank you,' Chelsea made herself say, watching with troubled eyes as Elaine walked away. If only she could think up some viable excuse and trot after her— the last thing she wanted was to be alone with Quinn.

But her wretched brain failed to come up with anything and he said, 'I'd like to talk to you. Let's find somewhere to sit, shall we?' And dropped an arm lightly around her shoulders.

Chelsea leapt as though stung by the contact, his lightest touch sending needle-sharp tremors scalding through her body and although his eyes revealed a momentary glint of anger he was grinning as he backed off, his hands lifted in a gesture of mock surrender, his voice taunting her.

'Look, no hands! I just want to talk, promise!'

What about? she wondered, following a pace behind him, her eyes wary. Surely they had said all that had to be said on the vexed subject of their so-called engagement.

If he wanted to grumble at her for getting him into this mess then she would give him a straight answer. She had involved him in the first place, and she was willing to take the blame for that, even though he had had the opportunity of saying an unequivocal, 'No'. No one had actually forced him to agree to her request. But he had brought the resulting publicity down on his own head. Besides, hadn't he said that it gave him the perfect let-out where the lovesick Sandy was concerned?

Still trying to figure out what he had on his mind, she watched him sink down on a sloping stretch of lawn which formed a natural partition between the green amphitheatre at the rear of the house and the secluded courtyard beyond where, beneath an attractive planting of flowering shrubs, she could see the greeny blue glitter of the swimming-pool.

Patting the grass beside him, he stretched out full length, his hands clasped behind his head. Sunlight revealed just a few strands of grey in the thick black hair cut close to his head and threw the aggressive jut of his cheekbones and jaw into stark prominence.

Flicking her eyes away from his totally arresting features, Chelsea lowered herself to the ground at a safe distance, her knees drawn up to her chin, and Quinn said, 'Peaceful, isn't it? I love this place. I only fully relax and unwind when I'm here.'

'You could have fooled me,' Chelsea couldn't help scorning. 'You always give the impression of being completely laid-back, taking life just the way it comes and enjoying it to the hilt.'

'Appearances can be deceptive.' He turned his head, his half-closed eyes brushing over her hunched, defensive position. 'Controlling Ryder-Gem, getting the best out of everyone involved, keeping growth sustainable, isn't a piece of cake. I keep on top of it,' he understated, 'but that doesn't mean I have to tread the earth at a run, teeth clenched and scowling, just to demonstrate what a high-flyer I am! However...' His eyes smiled into hers, making her stomach curl with a pleasure that went right down to her toes. The devil could charm a miser into parting with his gold and, unfortunately, he knew it. Flustered, she looked into the distance and heard him continue, 'I didn't want to talk about my job, but yours.'

And that did surprise her. In her admittedly jaundiced opinion she had imagined he gave women little real thought. When he thought about a woman at all it would be to wonder what she'd be like in bed, never delving beneath the surface, finding out what made her tick as a human being, looking on the female of the species as creatures expressly created for his pleasure.

'What do you want to know?' She could handle this; she knew her job backwards and was proud of the work she did, and he shifted, turning on to his side, resting his chin on his hand, the dark shirt he was wearing straining over his broad chest, his golden eyes alight with interest as he instructed,

'Everything. How you got started, how you ended up making commercials with Triple A. It's a highly regarded agency, so you must have more than fluff between your ears.'

'You can count on it!' Her deep blue eyes were laughing as she told him how, after leaving school with three A levels, she had taken a secretarial course, joined Triple A and gone on to night-school to improve her skills, climbing quickly through the secretarial hierarchy to the position of PA to the television director. How, during her time with Miles, she had learned every aspect of the filming of commercials, had developed her own impressive client list, and had ended up practically running the department.

'And the rest, you know,' she ended, completely relaxed now, her legs tucked beneath her, one hand idly plucking daisies. And Quinn levered himself up on one elbow, the look he gave her very direct.

'An impressive record. Complete dedication, I take it?'

Chelsea nodded a brisk affirmative. Her career was the only important thing in her life and she didn't regret it. She had planned it that way, schooling her emotions until they had ceased to exist. Because, if they didn't exist, they couldn't hurt her.

Quinn chewed reflectively on a grass stalk, his narrowed eyes intent on her features as he said, 'I don't understand why you allowed Robartes to push you into a corner. You have a direct mind for a woman; I would have thought you would have gone straight to the top with your application for promotion, and not through Robartes.'

A logical surmise, she thought snappily, clenching her teeth. His patronising reference to her mind being direct—for a woman—had flicked raw nerve-ends. And she said tightly, 'You're right. But you can't know our chairman, or you'd never suggest such a thing.' And at the interrogatory tilt of his strongly marked brows she explained more equably, 'Sir Leonard is the archetypal chauvinist; he doesn't regard women as suitable managerial material, let alone capable of holding their own at directorship level—and the position I'm after carries a directorship. I knew darned well that if I applied for Miles's job under my own steam he would refuse to consider me.' Abstractedly, she plucked a few more daisies, adding them to the dozen or so already clutched in her palm. 'But Miles, as they say, has his ear, and Miles knows I'm capable of stepping into his shoes. And I thought—quite naturally, I consider—that his recommendation to the chairman, plus my track record, would clinch it.'

'But he tried to use his influence to blackmail you into his bed.' Quinn lay on his back again, his eyes closed against the sun. 'That's an even worse form of chauvinism.'

'You blackmailed me into coming down here,' she reminded him, snatching at a few more daisies. In her opinion it was a case of the pot calling the kettle black, and she wasn't going to let him forget it!

'But I told you you wouldn't regret spending time here,' he countered easily, obviously incapable of seeing anything wrong in the way he had forced her to do as he wanted.

She wouldn't regret having known this place. Already, in the short time she'd spent here, the utter tranquillity, the timeless beauty had begun to weave its own special kind of magic. But she had a nasty suspicion that he had brought her here to seduce her—his explanation of their need to evade the gossip-hungry Press didn't stand up under close examination since he'd already put them off the scent with the story his Press officer had put out. And what had happened the moment he'd got her alone in her bedroom only served to strengthen the case against him—that, and the way he looked at her. And if she allowed herself to be seduced then that was something she would regret for the rest of her life.

As a lover he would be unforgettable—as many other women had probably discovered to their cost. And she wasn't prepared to face that kind of complication.

She was so lost in her tumultuous thoughts that when he next spoke she had to ask him to repeat himself, and he pulled himself into a sitting position, facing her.

'There are always other jobs, other opportunities. You could have told Robartes to get lost and moved to an agency where your talents would have been appreciated, and properly rewarded.'

He was perfectly serious. There was a snap, an intentness in his eyes she had never seen before, and he had an air of waiting for her response, as if it could be important. Chelsea shrugged, looking away because holding his eyes had an uncomfortable effect on her. She was afraid that her own expression might give her away, although she was unsure of exactly what there was to reveal.

'Why should I? I've made friends at Triple A, good ones. I've built up my own client list, I know what I'm doing and where I want to go.' She chewed hard on a corner of her full lower lip. 'Why should I go because the chairman's blinkered and Miles is without principle where his sex needs are concerned?'

She could feel the heat of anger building up inside her, an anger that had been there ever since Miles had made his degrading suggestion and she knew Quinn had picked it up when his voice came, soothingly husky.

'Don't let it get to you, Chelsea. You decided to fight it out—and even if the weapon you chose wasn't exactly orthodox you've got what you wanted.' He took the handful of daisies out of her nerveless fingers. 'Robartes, because he wants to get the Ryder-Gem account for Triple A—presuming, of course, that we dispense with our own advertising department—will put your promotion application right under your chairman's nose simply because he daren't fall foul of your future husband. Me. By the time the engagement is officially cancelled you will be installed as television director, confidently proving to all and sundry that they couldn't have appointed a better person for the job. And by that time, of course, Robartes will be out of the equation.'

She nodded, her head bent on the slender column of her neck. He had said exactly what she had repeatedly turned over inside her own head, drawing the same conclusions, and her lungs tightened with a sudden tiny intake of air as he lifted her head, one finger beneath her chin, because she thought he was going to kiss her again.

And, for a moment, she was sure he would, and was afraid of how she would react. But she began to tremble, terrified of herself, of her unpredictable response to this one man, and the moment was gone. She read the changed decision in the sudden cooling of his eyes, the entirely brotherly peck of a kiss which he perfunctorily dropped on the end of her nose, the way he crowned her head with the daisy-chain he'd been deftly making from the tiny blooms she'd so heedlessly mangled.

'Don't get so uptight, princess.' He got lithely to his feet, brushing blades of grass from his narrow-fitting cream-coloured trousers. 'Everything's going to turn out fine.' He held out a hand to help her to her feet, releasing it immediately, his voice friendly but definitely impersonal as he told her, 'Ma likes a cup of tea around this time. We'll make a pot. And as Mrs Cranforth isn't around I'll ferry us down to the local for a meal this evening. Nothing fancy, but it will save having to bother to cook for ourselves. It's too darn hot.'

It was still too hot, Chelsea thought, dragging the brush through her long black hair. Sticky heat. Despite her shower her skin felt clammy, her nightdress sticking to her.

Putting the brush down, she turned slowly. Her bedroom was as lovely as the rest of the house—which Elaine had toured her round before Quinn had taken them to the village pub, once a staging post for the routes into mid-Wales.

For the duration of her stay here she would be sleeping in a four-poster bed with rich brocade hangings, her room boasting genuine Sheraton furniture. At least, she thought it was genuine and, knowing Quinn Ryder, knowing of his wealth and single-mindedness, she guessed he would never be content with reproductions, no matter how good. He would never settle for second best.

But, no matter how appealing she found the idea of sleeping in a four-poster, she simply wasn't ready to settle down. It was well after midnight. She and Elaine had sat up talking when they'd returned from the village, and Quinn must have gone to his own room, she supposed, since she hadn't laid eyes on him since they'd come back into the house.

His own room. Right next to hers. For some reason that knowledge sent a strange *frisson* down her spine. Quickly walking to the open windows, she drew back the curtains and stared out into the darkness.

Since their talk this afternoon she had unwittingly found herself liking the man, feeling closer to him. Yet he, although behaving in an exemplary fashion throughout the evening, had seemed to draw back, as if deliberately distancing himself.

Too exemplary? He'd been nothing like the man she had become so wary of. To begin with, even though she'd tried to pretend it wasn't happening, he had let her know he found her desirable with every word, every look. And then, later, particularly after he'd kissed her, she had had to face that fact.

She leaned her elbows on the window-sill, pulling in lungfuls of scented night air. It hadn't been easy knowledge to face up to, particularly since she had been powerless to prevent herself from responding so wholeheartedly to him. And what had he called her, during that conversation? Uptight.

She shook her head in immediate denial. Of course she wasn't uptight! Except, she amended with painful honesty, when she was around him.

He was enough to give any right-minded woman the jitters—he had been born with far too much charm and that, coupled with his undeniable masculinity, was a pretty potent combination.

An owl gave a melancholy hoot from somewhere deep in the forest and Chelsea sighed, too restless, too edgy to begin to think of sleep. Her room overlooked the courtyard where, earlier, she had glimpsed the swimming-pool, and she straightened up, snapping herself together.

Pointless to get herself in a state over her relationship with Quinn. A relationship which was edgy at best and wouldn't last a moment longer than it took for Sandy to realise that she was fighting a lost cause. Pointless to live over and over in her head every look he had given her, trying to catch, in retrospect, every nuance of what he had said. Pointless even to think about him, let alone allow him to take over her mind!

Elaine had left Cassie's bikini on top of her bed, Chelsea had transferred it smartly to a drawer. Now she extracted it and tugged her sprigged cotton nightdress over her head.

Tonight, in this stifling heat, would be the perfect time to make use of that pool. The exercise would rid her of her edginess and the water would cool her down. And then she would sleep, quite dreamlessly.

Cassie had a daring taste in swimwear, she thought, surveying the minute triangle of scarlet fabric in the pier-glass. And a much smaller bust than her own, she decided, pulling a face as she clipped the front fastening of the sexily cut bra. With this wisp of nonsense the only swimwear on offer, she would make every excuse in the book to avoid appearing in it during the daytime. But at night, tonight, there would be no one around to see her.

It took her longer than she had expected to creep out of the house, treading very carefully, not wanting to wake the others, and she got lost twice trying to locate the pool, but when she found it she grinned with pleasure. It was well worth the effort!

The water was inviting, glinting softly in the shimmering light of the moon. Chelsea skirted a grouping of luxuriously padded loungers, balanced herself on the edge of the pool and dived in.

The sensation of cleaving through skin-soft, skin-warm water was exhilarating, and she swam underwater, her mind a primeval and blessed blank until she felt that her lungs were bursting, and soared upwards, breaking the surface with a cascade of bubbles, shaking her streaming hair out of her eyes.

'Couldn't you sleep either?' The deep, husky drawl froze her, and something kicked right down inside her, making her feel giddy, and, blinking water from her eyes, she had a blurred vision of a powerful male body, moonlight moulding taut muscles, before Quinn executed the perfect dive which brought him effortlessly to her side.

Treading water, she tried to get a grip on herself. She knew exactly the type of man he was—the complete sexual opportunist—and she should be able to control her witless response to him. But as he broke the surface beside her his body brushed hers and the sensation of skin on wet skin was more than she could bear and she knew she had to get out of here.

His eyes were black in the moonshadows, fathomless, mesmerising her, and she had to fight hard to manage, 'I'll go back in now. The pool's all yours.' She couldn't share it with him, run the gauntlet of his wicked eyes and clever hands. She couldn't. He possessed a brand of dark magic that made her feel things she didn't want to feel, had never expected to feel.

Determinedly, she pushed her way through the water and began to haul herself up the steps at the side of the pool, every muscle locking in shock as his firm hands grasped her hips, his long fingers tight against the soft sides of her stomach.

'I want you to stay.' His voice was an inescapable command, deep and warm yet denying disobedience, and Chelsea's bones went weak, her legs not strong enough to hold her as he pulled her back into the water, holding her hard against his body. He was wearing only the briefest of swimming-trunks and her breath clogged in her throat, her heart leaping and twisting like a crazy thing, hammering against her ribs as the now all-too-familiar heat of response turned her body to flame.

His powerful shoulders and chest were slicked with diamond-bright drops of water and her eyes were drawn with unwilling fascination to the black clusters of body hair lying against his tanned skin, and her breasts were throbbing, straining against the ineffectual scarlet covering as she ached to press herself against the hard wall of his chest, her soft lips parting in instinctive, unwitting, wanton invitation...

And he moved his head, taking her mouth with his, and the traitor within held her precisely where she was as his tongue stroked the inner corners of her mouth with wicked expertise, blocking out the warning censor in her mind.

The teasing, soft stroke of his tongue, shafting deeper, more intimately now, made her frantic for more, much more, and, without her realising it, her arms snaked around his neck, her body pressing instinctively closer to his, the chemical reaction that effectively obliterated common sense bonding her to him.

'Chelsea——' Her name was torn from him on a deep-throated groan as his kiss deepened to fierce possessiveness, and she could feel the slight tremor that shook his hands as they hungrily shaped her body and, even while her wantonly eager hands began to learn the impressively masculine contours of his back, he tore his mouth from hers, scooped her into his arms and waded towards the steps.

Afterwards, she would never be able to remember how they came to be lying on one of the padded loungers, his aroused body half covering hers. She shuddered in forbidden rapture as his hand moved slowly from the inviting swell of her breasts across the flat plane of her stomach to the soft flare of her hips.

Mindlessly, she held out her arms to him, folding them around his shoulders as his head came down, his lips trailing fiery sensation over her skin as they feathered down to the tiny, tantalising triangle between her thighs, and she caught her breath because she was drowning...drowning...

CHAPTER SIX

WITH a low, hoarse groan, Quinn straightened beside Chelsea, his hand resting lightly on her hip, the pads of his fingers burning into her sensitised skin, his breath coming fast, as fast as the shallow gasps that were making the firm fullness of her peaked breasts push erotically against the tiny scraps of damp scarlet fabric.

A low moan of husky protest at his sudden withdrawal emerged from her parted lips and he said, 'Easy. Easy, sweetheart,' and placed the warm palm of his hand on her breast, as if to steady the racing heartbeat beneath the curving, heated flesh. 'We have all the time in the world.'

Time for what? Time for loving, for love? But Quinn didn't love, did he? He had a cynical view of women and she—she had forsworn the emotion, hadn't she? She knew from bitter experience that love was painful. It chewed people up and spat them out and they were never the same again. She felt giddy, afraid of how easily he could change her viewpoint, and she found her voice and it came out thickly, on a whisper.

'No!'

His teeth gleamed briefly in his moon-shadowed face, and his voice was warm, heartbreakingly tender.

'But yes, believe me. I've wanted you since I first saw you.' Seductive fingers drifted slowly upwards, finding the frantic pulse-beat in the hollow at the base of her throat. 'I've ached to discover the real woman beneath that cool and lovely exterior. So, my eager little darling, if I can wait a little longer, so can you.'

He had misunderstood her completely! And she knew she should put him right, and be utterly firm about it, but his feather-light touch was creating havoc and she had lost the power of speech. She gave a tiny ravaged gasp as he bent his dark head and lightly brushed her lips with his then settled his formidable length beside her, his body searing her, igniting fires that were building up to a roaring conflagration.

He was supporting his head on one hand, the veiled glitter of his half-closed eyes a hypnotic threat, his other hand gently tracing the moon-blanched contours of her face, holding her in thrall.

'I couldn't believe my luck when you begged me to tell Robartes we were engaged,' he murmured, his voice laced with amusement. 'It had been as much as I could do to get you to pass the time of day with me before. And then you came, offering me the opportunity of a lifetime.'

His fingers were tracing the fragile line of her collarbone now and she dragged her gaze from his, focusing her eyes on the stars, brilliant points of light in the black velvet sky. She had to put an end to this honeyed seduction. She had to. Somehow.

'The opportunity to force me to come down here,' she dragged out at last, fighting the sensations he was creating within her body, her control not firm enough to keep her voice steady.

'As you say, my beautiful darling.' His voice thickened, darkened, as dark as the desires he aroused as his fingers stroked the deep cleft between her breasts, finding the front fastening of the inadequate scarlet bra, unclasping it with a subtle, expert movement.

Chelsea uttered a small smothered scream. There was more danger here than she had ever imagined possible. Fighting for control, she pushed herself up on her elbows, her whole body shaking with the effect of what he was doing to her.

But her ill-considered movement had been a mistake; she knew that as soon as his lips closed around one revealingly erect nipple, and then her mind gave way to utter delirium, totally incapable of doing battle with her clamouring senses. Rhythmically, he suckled her engorged ripeness, driving her insane, and she was pleading with him now, begging in a wild, lost whisper that she didn't recognise as her own.

And he lifted his head, his face hard and wanting in the ghostly moonlight, his voice all ragged edges, quick, insistent.

'I want you. Body and soul, I want you. Move in with me, be my woman. Go where I go, lie where I lie. Chelsea ... promise ...'

As his impassioned words shattered the sensory haze, Chelsea went very still. She swallowed convulsively, fighting the painful lump in her throat. He was asking her to be his mistress. Good God! Live with him. Until he tired of her. How long? A month? Two?

She was hurting. Why? Why should she be hurt when this was what she had expected all along? She knew exactly what type of man he was.

Twisting off the lounger, she made a grab for the towel she'd brought with her, wrapping it round her tautly held body with a single angry gesture.

She despised herself utterly, she really did. All of this mess was of her own making. Her instincts had been right; she should never have allowed him within ten yards of her! He would grab what was on offer with both hands, and she had known that. She shouldn't have offered!

'Calm down.' He was on his feet, right beside her, in only a little longer than the time it took her to draw breath. 'What's this all about, honey?' His tone was as soft as velvet. He must have been way ahead of the queue when they handed out self-assurance. She could almost see it oozing out of his pores.

Adroitly side-stepping, she evaded his outstretched hand. Did he think she was simple? That simple! She would never allow him to touch her again. She knew, to her shame, exactly what he could do to her.

She dragged in a shuddering breath. 'This is about——' she began in a voice as clipped as she knew how to make it '—about my refusal of your offer. I won't be your mistress.' Her chin jerked up. In allowing him to bewitch her out of her senses, his dark magic weaving a mind-blowing spell, she had unthinkingly embroiled herself in this appalling situation. And the only way to extricate herself with any dignity at all was to tell him, as clearly and concisely as she could, that she was not that type of woman!

If she ever made love with a man it would be because she loved him, was totally and eternally committed to him. And as falling in love was something she would never allow herself to do...

'No?' His voice had gone as hard as the ungiving planes of his face. 'Holding out for marriage? Saving yourself until you've pushed the price as high as it will go?'

'Marriage!' Her voice came out with a shrillness that surprised her. But his taunt had been unforgivable. Too incensed to guard her tongue, she snapped out, 'Marriage is the last thing on my mind. I'm not stupid, I've seen what it can do to people.'

'Nice try.' He clearly didn't believe her, and the cynical curl of his mouth infuriated her into shouting,

'If you'd watched your parents fight, verbally tear each other to shreds, ever since you were old enough to know what was going on—if you'd seen your own sister's marriage fall apart as soon as the honeymoon period was over and the hard reality of day-to-day living set in—you'd think twice before you walked into that trap! But I was forgetting——' her eyes anointed him with bitterness '—you'd think twice, more than twice. You think every woman is after your precious money!'

Blindly, she stepped back, away from the cold blast of anger she could sense in him, see in the biting glitter of his eyes, in the hard jut of his facial bones. But she wasn't finished with him. Not yet. Not quite.

Turning in a wild flurry of flying hair, she bit out, 'I wouldn't marry you if you came with million-pound notes sticking out of both ears!' and fled, tears of rage scalding her face.

*   *   *

She was calmer in the morning. Much calmer. She had slept hardly at all, shame and self-disgust making uncomfortable pillow-partners.

But at least she was clearer in her mind. She'd shrieked at Quinn like a fishwife, but he had deserved it, hadn't he? And at least he would be under no more illusions where her availability—or lack of it—was concerned.

So they knew where they stood.

Careful attention to make-up went some way to disguising the shadows under her eyes and, rummaging through the mostly casual clothes she'd brought along, she'd teamed a black, fully gathered fine cotton skirt with a short-sleeved, conventionally styled white shirt.

After what had happened last night it would be impossible to stay on here, she rationalised, twisting round in front of the mirror to check that no stray strands of glossy dark hair escaped the confines of her chignon. Quinn, of course, would be only too ready to agree. He had only brought her here in order to seduce her, persuade her to become his mistress—that much he had openly admitted.

Now he knew she had no intention of doing any such thing he would be only too happy to see the back of her. He could think up something to explain her sudden departure to his mother and Chelsea was beyond caring whether the story he concocted was believed or not.

Coming face to face with Quinn, after the utterly abandoned way she'd behaved last night, was not going to be easy, she knew that. But faced he must be. And soon, before her nerve failed her altogether.

Pushing her feet into plain black pumps with medium heels, she left her room, walking firmly along the gallery and down the stairs, determined to handle the coming confrontation with cool dignity.

It was not quite half-past seven, and she was praying that Elaine was not an early riser. As for Quinn, well, she'd heard the bad-tempered slam of the adjoining bedroom door barely twenty minutes ago and knew he'd be around somewhere.

She ran him to earth in the huge, low-beamed country kitchen, sitting at the central pine table, his head buried in the morning paper, his back to a big, shiny red electric Aga.

He didn't look up and the sight of his endlessly out-stretched legs, the dark blue denim fabric moulding his thighs, made Chelsea's stomach twist over. Ignoring the unpleasant manifestation as best she could, she cleared her throat and clipped out, 'I would like to leave. I can be packed in ten minutes, which should give you ample time to phone for a taxi to run me to the nearest station.'

For what seemed like hours he didn't move. And then the paper was slowly lowered and he stared at her blankly as if he didn't know who she was.

'Why?' he asked coolly, his features as expressionless as a stone. 'We agreed you'd stay here for two weeks. You've been here less than twenty-four hours.'

He lifted the paper again, putting a barrier between them, dismissing her. But Chelsea had no intention of being dismissed, no intention of staying under the same roof as Quinn, for that matter.

'I agreed to nothing,' she pointed out tartly. 'You in-sisted. Threatened, in fact. And if I'm leaving then why don't you ask yourself whose fault that is?'

The newspaper didn't even twitch and Chelsea clamped her teeth together and slowly counted to ten. She, who had always prided herself on her ability to stay cool and collected in circumstances which would send others running round in circles, could feel herself going to pieces, out of control, her temper rising to undreamed-of heights. Never before had she encountered anyone who could reduce her to a mass of intense emotions—emotions, moreover, over which she had precious little control.

The sooner she removed herself from his orbit, the better. And she informed the upraised newspaper snippily, 'If you won't phone for a taxi, then I will.' And she sucked in her breath as he hurled the paper into a corner of the room and jack-knifed to his feet, his eyes furious.

'You'll do no such thing. You'll stay right here.' His voice bit into her soul, making her flinch, and she didn't know which was harder to cope with—his bitter anger, his cold indifference, his flirtatious charm or his devastating passion.

Cursing herself for her lack of foresight in not simply sloping away without alerting him to her intentions, she managed to meet his quelling gaze unflinchingly, managed to ask him witheringly, 'What's the point? You'd thrown the Press off the scent even before we came here—so that excuse won't hold water. You only wanted me here to seduce me.'

She closed her eyes briefly against the entirely unwelcome sensation that spiralled around inside her as she recalled how very nearly he had achieved just that, then tossed bitterly, 'I won't be your mistress, you know that. I don't go in for casual relationships——' she almost quailed as she caught the cynical downtwist of his lips, the gleam of derision in his eyes but forced herself on because this was something she had to make him understand '—and before you so gallantly accuse me of holding out for marriage I'm telling you I don't go in for permanent relationships either. So am I making that phone call? Or are you?'

'Neither.' His tone was sharp enough to cut through stone and he walked to the door, his spine rigid with controlled fury. 'If you reappear at your apartment or place of work, people will talk. We're supposed to be behaving like a newly engaged couple, doing what comes naturally on a tropical island. You stay. I'll leave.'

The door banged behind him with a reverberation that seemed to shake the house on its foundations and, after one still moment, Chelsea shot over the floor, dragging the door open and flinging at his retreating back, 'And what good will that do? People will still talk, put two and two together!' She was so enraged, she didn't know herself. For some insane reason, the fact that he was walking out on her, leaving her behind had made her more furious than she had ever been in her life before. And he turned, his cold yellow eyes raking her angry face with chilling scorn.

'I, at least, know how to be discreet. No one will know I'm not where I'm supposed to be.'

Chelsea watched him turn on his heel and disappear through a door which led into the main hall, conquering the impulse to run after him, to beat her fists against that broad, unyielding chest, making herself walk back into the kitchen on legs that were displaying a treacherous tendency to give way.

It was a peculiar kind of chemistry, she informed herself when she had got the riotous impulses of her brain back under some sort of control. That was all. Wearily, she slid the huge black kettle on to the Aga hotplate and waited for it to boil for tea. Now that her anger had drained away she felt more tired than she could ever remember, the events of last night and this morning taking their emotional toll.

Sitting at the table, sipping the hot, reviving tea, she did her best to put everything into perspective. Normally, she was completely level-headed, but she had been on edge ever since Miles Robartes had made his disgusting blackmail attempt. And her brainwave, her solution, while solving the Robartes problem, had backfired, giving Quinn Ryder all the leverage he required.

And that had put her even more on edge. And, given his shattering male potency, it had been little wonder that her celibate body had overridden her logical brain and responded to the sensual male in him as a parched blossom would respond to the rain. And her unreasoning anger because he was leaving was merely the physical manifestation of her self-disgust at the way she had behaved last night. A simple chemical equation, that was all.

Besides, she rationalised, she was glad he was leaving. This charming house, coupled with Elaine's uncomplicated company, was just what she needed. Here, in this benign tranquillity, without Quinn's utterly shattering presence, she would be able to recover the emotional stability which he, like a thief, could take from her with such devastating ease.

'What on earth have you done to my son?' Elaine's pleasant voice was lightly coloured with amusement and Chelsea looked up as her hostess entered the kitchen, and closed the door quietly behind her. And Chelsea forced herself to smile, hoping it didn't come over as a snarl, a baring of teeth that contained little goodwill and no spontaneity. 'Fresh tea? Oh, good.' Elaine helped herself from the pot and Chelsea's spine went stiff with tension.

Quinn's mother was no fool and she could only hope that the older woman would be tactful enough to let the subject drop. But nothing, it seemed, would go right for her today because as Elaine joined her at the table she imparted, 'Even as a small boy, Quinn never lost his temper. His father and I always swore he was born knowing how to get his own way by other, more appealing means. Of course, that kind of completely self-assured charm can be dangerous.'

Elaine lifted her teacup, her eyes twinkling into Chelsea's studiously blank ones. 'When the formula that has worked like a dream for thirty-six years is suddenly shown to be ineffective then it comes as a nasty shock. Bound to create a feeling of impotency, a display of bad temper.'

Elaine carefully replaced her cup in its saucer and lifted her shoulders in a delicate shrug. 'And boy, was he in a temper when he informed me he was on his way to Birmingham International to get a flight to Amsterdam! Apparently, he will be staying for an unspecified length of time with a diamond merchant and his wife who,' she explained, 'apart from being a close business associate, is perhaps his oldest and best friend. So, I repeat my question, what on earth did you do to him? What went wrong?'

Chelsea stared at the dregs in her teacup, feeling grim, in no mood for lengthy explanations, or evasions. She could point out that Quinn's unusual foul temper was down to plain old-fashioned sexual frustration and agree that, yes, the experience of having a woman he fancied turn him down flat must have been salutary, and give a seasoned opinion that he would get over it in next to no time because passion, for him, was a fleeting and elusive thing, like a half-remembered dream and, like a dream, would soon be forgotten completely.

Instead, she said tightly, 'From what you say, I take it you knew he had brought me here to seduce me?' And wondered how she'd had the gall to say such a thing to the man's own mother, and mentally flinched, expecting a well-deserved verbal slap, her eyes widening with surprise when Elaine gave a genuine gurgle of laughter and told her,

'You make me sound like a procuress! More tea?' She refilled both their cups, her movements very relaxed. 'No, I knew Quinn had brought you here because you were someone special. He doesn't share this place with anyone, other than family. He's very much a family man, did you know that?' A delicate brow was raised in Chelsea's direction. 'It's a pity he never married, he'd make a wonderful father, but he had a particularly harrowing experience when he was in his very early twenties. She behaved extremely badly—and, well, since then, he's never taken a woman seriously.'

Chelsea drank her tea in thoughtful silence. She was going to have to watch her tongue. She liked Elaine and wasn't going to hurt her by telling her that her beloved son had become so hard and cynical that he didn't care how he treated his women. He obviously must have led the besotted Sandy a long way up the garden path, for instance, and had grasped the opportunity of the false engagement not to help her, Chelsea, out of a tight corner, but to rid himself of the now unwanted lover in the cruellest way possible. Let his mother keep some illusions.

But she had to say something to indicate that she wasn't rudely ignoring the other woman's confidences and so she forced a level of lightness into her voice and chided, 'I am in no way special, as you put it. Quinn brought me here because he had no option if he wanted to avoid our being hounded by the Press.'

Elaine laughed openly as she collected the used teacups and put them in the dishwasher.

'If you say so, dear. But I've yet to see Quinn run and hide from anyone, least of all the gentlemen of the Press. But if it comforts you to think that way, go right ahead! Now——' she reached into the fridge for bacon '—breakfast. And then I suggest we leave all the boring chores for the devoted Ellie Cranforth while I show you around some of our glorious countryside. It's a beautiful day and I promise I won't spoil it for you by mentioning that rapscallion son of mine one more time. My lips, as they say, are sealed on that particular subject from now on!'

*   *   *

The day was beautiful, and it was followed by another and yet another until a week had slipped by. Walking with Elaine, helping her garden under the suspicious and possessive eye of Jerry Meakes, basking in the sun at the side of the swimming-pool gave Chelsea an enviable tan which accentuated the deep blue of her eyes and disguised the shadows beneath that were a direct legacy of sleepless nights.

Hauling herself out of the pool, out of breath following the strenuous efforts of the last half-hour, the pace she had set herself, she towelled herself dry and began to rub sun-screen on to all exposed parts. No matter how she tried to exhaust herself she still found night-time a wakeful, miserable experience.

Keeping her promise, Elaine had never once mentioned Quinn and had proved to be a delightful companion and, under the influence of this beautiful old house and its environs, Chelsea had begun to really relax. Until she was on her own, that was. And then she simply couldn't get Quinn out of her head.

She hadn't known she could be so stupid.

The rays of the sun were powerful enough to dry the disgraceful bikini almost immediately and, for modesty's sake, she covered it with a pair of brief white shorts and a sleeveless black cotton shirt.

Elaine always rested for a couple of hours after lunch, recharging her batteries, and, during that time, Chelsea had made a point of keeping herself occupied. Swimming, and, after that, gardening or walking. But today it was too darned hot to do anything so she dragged one of the loungers into the shade of a flowering shrub and reached for her sunglasses and a book, determined to keep her mind occupied.

But the memories of him reached right inside her head, clinging there, refusing to go away. Chelsea groaned in despair, pushed her sunglasses to the top of her head and knuckled her eyes. She was missing the brute; there was a hopeless ache deep down inside her, a sense of permanent loss, and she didn't understand herself at all because, by now, starved of his tantalising presence, her wretched hormones should have settled down to normal, because that aberration had been nothing more serious, or permanent than plain lust.

Yet still he invaded her mind, pushing in where he had no right to be, and she remembered his words, 'Be my woman, go where I go, lie where I lie...' and her heart twisted sickeningly inside her, thumping against her breastbone, and she was lonely, so desperately lonely...

Abruptly, she swung her feet to the paving slabs, stuffing them into strappy canvas shoes. Lying around here, without the distraction of Elaine's easy conversation, had been a stupid mistake. No wonder she couldn't get him out of her head when this was where he had done his best to seduce her—and had almost succeeded!

She would go and demand to be allowed to help Ellie in the kitchen, or Jerry Meakes in the garden, anything to occupy her stupid mind! And she heard Elaine say, 'Where are you off to in such a tearing hurry?'

She was standing at the top of the steps that led down to the paved pool surround, carrying a tray with two glasses, a jug.

'Ellie made lemonade. It's crammed with ice and I thought you'd like some.'

'Love some.' Chelsea bounded up the steps, taking the tray and carrying it down. No longer alone, she could push Quinn if not right out of her mind, at least to the back of it. 'I was just wondering if there was anything I could do around the kitchen?'

'Not a thing.' Elaine lowered herself on to a lounger, accepting the lemonade Chelsea had poured her. 'Ellie's gone, I told her to call it a day. You can rustle up one of those delicious salads you're so good at later, when it's cool enough to think of eating. And by the way, I'll be starting for Norfolk early tomorrow morning to stay with Erica until the new baby comes.' She swirled the liquid around in her glass, making the ice cubes tinkle. 'We'd arranged for me to go there before returning to Paris, but I was about to phone and change the plans— at least for another week. But Quinn called me from Amsterdam to say he'll be back here by lunchtime tomorrow, so I can go with a clear conscience. I'd have felt guilty if I'd left you to spend the second half of your stay here on your own. But, as things turned out, Quinn will be around to entertain you.' She smiled complacently. 'So that's all right, and everything's settled.'

And Chelsea stared at her, her small face set, pale under the bloom of her tan. Everything was far from being 'all right' and the only thing that was settled was her own immediate departure! Having Quinn around to 'entertain' her was something she was too cowardly to contemplate!

CHAPTER SEVEN

AND Elaine picked that up because at eight-thirty the following morning she said, 'I never thought you'd be a coward, but yes, if you insist, I'll drop you off at the station.'

Chelsea had been up very early, her packed bags in the hall, Elaine's favourite breakfast of crisply grilled bacon and tomatoes ready and waiting.

'I can't stay. And don't ask me why,' she'd stated as she saw Elaine's brows shoot up. 'If you could drop me at the nearest station I'd be grateful. But if it's going to take you out of your way I'll phone for a taxi, if I may.'

'And how is Quinn going to feel about that?' Elaine had buttered a slice of toast, her voice very calm. 'He's expecting to find you here. You know that, of course.'

To renew his attempts at seduction, Chelsea had confirmed to herself. His fit of pique over, he was ready to try again. And this time he wouldn't take no for an answer. Wouldn't need to, she thought, cringing inwardly with self-disgust. But she wasn't going to be around, was she? And she clipped out, 'Then his expectations will be thwarted. I'll leave him a note.'

And that she had. Very terse and to the point, leaving it on the table, propped up against the fruit bowl where he couldn't fail to see it.

And apart from the comment about cowardice, made as Elaine drove her Metro through the woodland drive, nothing more was said on the subject until she drew up on the forecourt of Shrewsbury station.

'I think you're making a big mistake.' The older woman turned sideways in her seat, her yellow eyes warm. 'But it won't make a jot of difference to the outcome. I know my son, probably better than you do. Definitely better than you do if you think that by running away you have any hope of escaping!' And then, more seriously, 'I've never seen Quinn look at a woman the way he looked at you. It was a mixture of protectiveness, need and plain aggravation, so I think I was right when I said he regards you as someone special.'

Elaine was seeing what she wanted to see. In past conversations she had made it plain that she longed to see her son settled, married and raising a family. She was blinkered, refusing to acknowledge that wedded bliss was the last thing Quinn would let himself in for, that he believed every woman he came in contact with was primarily interested in his money.

Chelsea shifted in her seat. She longed to ask what had happened, way back in his past, to give him such a jaundiced opinion of the female sex, but she bit back the questions that were tumbling on the edge of her tongue because the less she knew about the real Quinn Ryder, the better. But didn't the idiot know that wealth and financial security would be the very last things any woman would think of when he was around?

'Are you sure you wouldn't like to change your mind? I can take you straight back to Monk's Norton, no trouble at all.'

Elaine's softly spoken query cut through her anguished thoughts and she pulled herself together, unsnapping her seatbelt, trying to smile.

'Quite sure, thank you. And thank you for coming out of your way—as I'm quite certain you did.' She was scrabbling for her handbag in the well of the car, her heart pounding because, for some weird reason, she ached to take up Elaine's offer. Actually physically ached.

And the older woman said firmly, halting her frantic fumblings with the door release, 'I believe I know you well enough to say you're a fastidious woman. I just want to tell you that Quinn is not the womaniser the more lurid of the tabloids make him out to be.' A smile crinkled the corners of her eyes. 'If for no other reason than he simply would not have had the time to indulge in the sexual adventures that have been attributed to him! When he took over the running and management of Ryder-Gem, on his father's death, the company wasn't what it is today. It was run-down, going nowhere except out. For years, until he wrestled it back to the top level of financial solidity, he literally did the work of ten men. Think about it.'

Chelsea did. As she carried her bags into the booking hall she thought about what Elaine had said and categorically dismissed it as so much wishful thinking on the part of his doting parent. Elaine didn't know about the two blondes and the redhead and, no matter what the pressure of work, Quinn always made time to relax. He'd said so himself and, in any case, Chelsea had the evidence of her own two eyes.

*   *   *

Determined to put him out of her mind and get on with her life, Chelsea went back to work, parried questions about the way she'd cut her holiday short, about the wedding plans, with vague answers which, thankfully, seemed to satisfy. And she tried not to flinch whenever the phone on her desk or back at her apartment rang out, tried not to wonder why he hadn't phoned in a blistering rage or followed her back to town to insist that she return with him to Monk's Norton.

But when one week and then two had elapsed and Quinn Ryder might as well have been inhabiting a different planet Chelsea congratulated herself on the fact that he had obviously given up on her, decided that pursuing her wasn't worth the expenditure of that sort of effort and that the next and only time she would hear from him would be when he contacted her to say it was safe to announce publicly that the engagement was off.

And wondered why she felt so depressed.

'Can you spare a moment?' Miles Robartes slid into her office and Chelsea lifted her head from the work on her desk. It wasn't like Miles to come to her; if he'd wanted to speak to her in the past he'd always demanded she go to him, no matter how busy and pushed for time she was. Yet since her return he had been like a fawning dog and she didn't have to be a genius to know why.

Now he was smiling, rubbing his hands together, and his voice was unctuous as he told her, 'One of your fiancé's secretaries phoned me just now with a message from him, reminding you not to forget your dinner date this evening.' Misunderstanding the way she sharply sucked in her breath, her eyes widening in shocked disbelief, he expounded, 'Obviously, since you're combining the pleasure of dining together with exploratory discussions on the possibility of his company using our advertising services, he thought it only ethical to pass the message through me.' He straightened his tie, brushing his immaculate lapels with the backs of his fingers, looking important. 'I, after all, was the one to make the initial approach. Ryder obviously appreciates that; hence the reminder through me. Although I'm sure you were in no danger at all of forgetting!'

Chelsea ignored his leer, turning back to her work, her eyes unseeing, although Miles couldn't know that as he murmured something about leaving her to it. But as soon as she heard the door close behind him she jerked to her feet, pacing the small room with rapid strides, her arms crossed, hugging her body.

Quinn Ryder was a sneaky, devious swine. He would have known that, had he asked, she would have turned down any and every invitation of his, known that she was determined not to have anything more to do with him and his wretched strategy for seduction. Hence the 'reminder' of a dinner date that had never been made, through Miles Robartes, with the business discussion bit tacked on as bait because Quinn would know that Robartes would, quite literally, rub his hands with glee over the thought of capturing the Ryder-Gem account, and would demand an exhaustive run-down on every last detail of the meeting.

Very clever! But not, she decided with characteristic firmness, quite clever enough!

He was selfishly obsessed with getting his own way but this time she was going to show him that he had bitten off more than he could chew when he'd decided to manipulate her!

Her mind made up, she dialled the number of the Ryder-Gem offices here in London and only by firmly stating her false status as the future Mrs Ryder did she get past the defensive battery of secretaries and PAs.

'I am not having dinner with you tonight—or ever,' she gritted out the moment he'd laconically given his name. 'And if you're genuinely interested, which I doubt, in using the services of the agency, then I suggest you wine and dine Miles Robartes.' Then added snidely, 'The pair of you have so much in common, I just know you'll both have a lovely time.'

And just how much they had in common was enough to shock her into an open-mouthed silence when he parried softly, 'Then am I to take it that you've had your position of TV director confirmed?' And then, following the complete silence from her end, 'Apparently not. I suggest you think it over. I'll pick you up at eight.'

She wore an understated little black dress, her only adornment a fine gold chain around her neck, her hair screwed back from her face, her make-up minimal. But even so she fumed as she gave herself a critical appraisal in her bedroom mirror; she looked like a starry-eyed adolescent embarking on her first date.

Nothing could disguise the melting expression in her huge, slightly slanting deep blue eyes or make the lush curves of her mouth less vulnerably soft. Or stop the trip of her heartbeat, which was irregularly interrupting its normal rhythm.

She was such a fool. She despaired of herself, she really did. Quinn had manipulated her, yet again, leaving her in no doubt that if she had completely refused to see him this evening he would say the few words to Miles Robartes that would see her career prospects bite the dust.

But in spite of that, in spite of what had happened—or very nearly happened—at Monk's Norton, her whole body ached for his touch just as her soul ached for a single precious moment in his presence.

The best thing she could do, she told herself with unwilling sagacity, was to get the hell out of the whole awful mess before she found herself mindlessly giving way to all his demands, becoming his lover for as long as he needed her.

The escape route was in her own hands, she acknowledged bleakly as she scooped up her black evening purse and walked through into her sitting-room to await his arrival.

She could find another job—probably not as good as her position with Triple A, especially with her promotion prospects and a directorship in the offing, but something to get her teeth into. And she could find another place to live. Slip out of Quinn's orbit forever.

Suddenly, her eyes filled with tears and she blinked them away crossly. Of course she was upset, she excused herself. The idea of having to look for another job, probably ending up with something much less high-powered, leaving the small but prestigious home she had taken such a pride in, was enough to upset anyone. So she wouldn't do it. She simply had to be strong, resist

Quinn's sexual importunings with every ounce of strength and will-power she had!

Her neat chin came up and it stayed that way as the doorbell announced his arrival. She snatched the door open, determined to treat him with the cool indifference he deserved, but just seeing him, his tall, magnificent body clothed with dark, elegant perfection, his sexy mouth curving with the very faintest of smiles, made her heart loop the loop, weakened her bones, made her realise just how much she had missed him...missed him...

Lazy amber eyes drifted with enigmatic appraisal over her body, compounding the confusion of her clamouring senses and she grabbed the white wool jacket she'd put ready over the back of the chair and marched out of the flat, banging the door behind her, and made a hurried rush for the lifts.

'Where's the fire?'

The deep dark velvet of his voice sent shudders down her spine and she couldn't tell him that she didn't trust herself alone with him so she informed him tartly, 'This evening wasn't my idea and I'd like to get it over with as soon as possible.' Which was hardly gracious, she conceded wryly, but was a fair excuse for the way she'd leapt for the lift.

Besides, she exonerated herself as the small satin-steel box whispered down to the underground parking space, normal politeness didn't enter the equation, not when dealing with a man who was prepared to use every devious method in the book to get his own way. And after he'd settled her into the gleaming BMW, taken his own place behind the wheel, he said softly, a slight hint of menace making her catch her breath, 'I haven't decided whether to forgive you for running out on me.'

'I'm heartbroken!' she came back sarcastically, and stared straight ahead through the windscreen, close to hitting him when his low chuckle of amusement threatened an intimacy she couldn't afford to admit. His very nearness in the confines of the car had a highly unsettling effect; it would be so easy to give in, succumb to the dark magic of his enchantment . . .

But she knew where that would lead, didn't she? Emotional involvement without long-term commitment was out, as far as she was concerned. She had too much respect for her body to give way to the transitory desires of the flesh and a long-term commitment was something she wasn't prepared to make because she knew the type of pain and humiliation that could follow. Besides, Quinn had also admitted that, for him, a permanent relationship was about the last thing he was looking for. So she would simply have to hold on to her common sense with both hands and constantly remind herself that passion did not last, that it quickly burned itself out, leaving bitterness behind.

Remind herself too that no matter how damned attractive, how utterly charming, beneath the skin he was no different from Miles Robartes, only interested in getting his own way and not averse to using blackmail to achieve his aims!

So, she would begin the evening as she intended it should continue, show him that he couldn't manipulate her, that if he was looking for a softening in her attitude, a return to the abandoned creature she had shown herself to be at the poolside that night, then he wouldn't find it.

'As I recall, it was you who left Monk's Norton, not me,' she pointed out levelly, her voice clipped and satisfactorily impersonal. 'Did you really imagine I would wait, panting with anticipation, for your return?'

And that husky, dangerous chuckle came again, making the colour fly to her face as he came back, 'If my imagination had stretched to conjuring up such an erotic image, I would have been back a damned sight sooner! But the day will come, gorgeous, it will come.'

He was incorrigible, totally infuriating, and she said crossly, 'Don't hold your breath!'

And he negotiated the fast-flowing traffic with consummate ease, telling her, 'And we both know why I left, don't we?' And he went on to elucidate when she would have much preferred not to hear this. 'If I'd stayed I would have ended up refusing to take your "No" for an answer. You wanted me as much as I wanted you, but you weren't ready to admit it.' His voice lowered to a husky, smoky caress. 'And I want you to admit it, freely, ask me for the pleasure you know damn well I can give you. When we make love—as we will, my pet— it's going to be perfect, the logical and honest outcome of the way we both feel.'

He turned the car into a relatively quiet square, tall, gracious town houses facing a small oasis of greenery, and Chelsea's throat closed up, her heart a frantic wild thing, beating against the cage of her ribs, making a fierce denial of his words impossible. And as he braked the BMW at the kerb outside one of the buildings he turned to her, his golden eyes drifting over the hectic flush of her skin, her tense, perfect profile, his voice little more than a whisper.

'Which is why we're eating out. My instincts were to feed you at the penthouse, but I knew I wouldn't be able to keep my hands off you. And we, my pet, have some talking to do first.'

Her whole body was trembling when he cupped a hand beneath her elbow as they mounted the steps beneath a discreet black and white awning to the exclusive restaurant he'd chosen. His honeyed tongue could charm the birds out of the trees—and the woman he wanted into his bed—but knowing that, repeating it firmly to the logical part of her brain, was having little effect. She decided she was going mad!

But she wasn't. Of course she wasn't, she informed herself staunchly as someone took her white jacket. The fever that was infecting her brain could be cured by a dose of straight thinking. He wasn't going to be allowed to seduce her with his silver words; she would set the tone, put the conversation on to a manageable plane.

The table they were shown to was more secluded than she would have liked, the lighting too soft, the single red rose in a crystal stem-vase too romantic. But she wasn't prepared to allow such trappings to deter her. And before he could say a word she whisked a notepad from her purse, uncapped her pen, fixed a businesslike expression on her face and suggested, 'Suppose you outline your thoughts on the possibility of Triple A taking the Ryder-Gem account on board? I'll take notes.'

And he shook his head, his eyes unfathomable in the hazy light of the candle which glimmered on the table between them, and gently took the notepad from her suddenly unresisting hands, putting it away in an inside pocket.

'I have no thoughts. Or only thoughts of you. I want you, Chelsea—but then, you know that. But it's more than that.'

Her eyes widened at his audacity and his gaze slid down to fasten on the frantic pulse-beat at the base of her throat, his voice quite level as he told her, 'I believe in honesty in all things, especially in the type of relationship we're going to share.' Champagne was brought to the table and he waved the waiter away with an abrupt slice of his hand, pouring the wine himself, and Chelsea knew he'd had this arranged: the most secluded table in the room, the absence of waiters requiring their orders, the wine appearing on cue.

He intended to sweet-talk his way through her defences, make love to her with words, get her relaxed and receptive with the aid of quantities of vintage champagne. She was, she recognised with much agitation, watching a master at work!

And she tried to harden her heart.

'If you're not going to discuss the agency, then what am I supposed to pass on to Miles in the morning?' she demanded with cool logic. Her slender fingers closed around her evening purse as she shifted her chair away from the table, informing him, 'And that being the case, I'm leaving.'

Steel fingers manacled her wrists, forcing her down again.

'To hell with Robartes—and the agency. Why don't you admit that you knew damn well I didn't bring you here to discuss advertising campaigns?'

She couldn't meet his eyes, outstare him, as every instinct demanded she do, lie through her teeth and tell him he was wrong. She had known. She had. He released her wrist and she rubbed the slightly reddened skin without knowing she was doing it. Maybe he was right. And maybe the only way to deal with this man was with total honesty.

'So tell me, what was your parents' reaction to the Press coverage of our so-called engagement?'

His light question took her by surprise, eased the strain, and if she was going to be completely honest with him she could start now. She had no hang-ups about her childhood; it had led her to where she was now— dedicated to her career, going places fast.

Absently, she lifted her glass, sipping the deliciously cold liquid and informed him drily, 'I doubt if they even remember my name, so the Press coverage wouldn't have meant a thing.' And saw the sudden flicker deep in his glorious eyes, saw the indentations harden at the side of his mouth and immediately regretted her flippancy. She apologised.

'I'm sorry, that's not quite the truth. But I haven't seen or heard of my father for twelve years. I was fourteen, Joannie twelve, when my parents finally divorced and he took off.'

'Joannie being your sister? And neither of you ever heard from him again?'

She nodded, 'Correct on both counts.' And he topped up her glass and held it by the stem, twisting it round, watching the foaming bubbles, hearing the soft compassion in his voice as he asked, 'Did you miss him? Did his desertion of you hurt that much?'

She toyed with the idea of asking him what he meant by 'that much' but decided not to bother, telling him honestly, 'No. I think we were more relieved than anything. At least there was an end to the terrifying rows and we knew our mother would be home on a permanent basis, not driven by Dad's infidelities into packing her bags and leaving. She always came back, after a few days or so, but we were never sure if she'd be there in the morning when we woke up.'

'And your mother—how did she take it?' Quinn prompted and Chelsea shrugged.

'She cried a lot. But then she is one of those women who needs a man around—even if he's no good. She needs to be part of a couple.' She glanced up at Quinn, her head tilted on one side. 'Some women can't cope on their own.'

'But you can,' he put in softly, a smile tugging at his mouth, not waiting for her affirmative. 'So, where is she now? You implied that neither of your parents took an interest in you now.'

Quinn's signal to a waiter was low-key but the food was brought to their table immediately. Poached langoustines with aiuoli sauce. How did he know it was one of her favourite dishes, the subtle flavour of the fresh Dublin Bay prawns enhanced by the rich garlicky sauce? Did their tastes dovetail that well? And he was waiting for an answer to his earlier question and she might as well supply it because talking about her uninspiring past was keeping his mind off more intimate topics.

'When the crying was over she began to come to life again. Joannie and I endured three separate "uncles". But when I was twenty-one she announced she was

leaving. The house we lived in in Stepney was sold and
the proceeds divided between Joannie and me. Mum had
found a rich and doting Italian. Vito's a widower, apparently extremely wealthy. I only met him once; he's
short and stout and almost bald.' She speared the last
of her prawns, not for one moment willing to betray
how disgusted she'd been.

Her mother had been still beautiful and she'd been
willing to sell herself for a luxurious lifestyle, a portly
lover who was happy to take all life's little upsets on his
own stout shoulders. 'He likes to travel a lot and Mum
goes with him.' She dabbed her mouth with the pale sage
napkin that exactly matched the tablecloth. 'The last time
I heard from her was a scrawled postcard from Sydney
six months ago. Vito, it seems, has a married daughter
in Australia.'

'So you embarked on adult life determined to be as
unlike your clinging-vine mother as possible,' Quinn remarked, almost to himself, as he filled her empty glass.
He had drunk sparingly, she noted, while she had dis-
posed of most of the bottle. But she didn't feel even
slightly tipsy, merely relaxed, able to talk freely about
the things she'd locked away years ago.

But she wasn't relaxed enough to tell him the complete truth, that, far from actively setting out to be totally
self-sufficient, she had actually sought a partner,
someone to love, someone to share her life with. So she
simply nodded a silent affirmation and began to eat the
delicious wild strawberries that had been placed in front
of her.

'You had a rotten time, one way or another, but you
can't let your father's desertion, and, to a lesser extent,

your mother's, ruin your whole life,' Quinn said firmly and Chelsea went rigid with a fury that was out of proportion to his words, her spoon poised halfway to her mouth.

Putting her spoon down carefully, she told him tightly, 'Ruin it? If I deliberately chose a career over marriage, why should that ruin my life?' She couldn't imagine now why she had told him as much as she had. She had never confided in anyone as much as she had just confided in him. She was a private person and was deeply regretting not having walked out, as she'd threatened, earlier. His belief that every woman should have a man in her life, and put that man before all else before she could be complete, was typically male. And she expounded tautly, 'A worthwhile career can be just as rewarding as marriage—far more rewarding as a matter of fact!'

'I wasn't talking about marriage,' he said with a flick of a smile that made her want to hit him. 'There can be other emotional involvements between the sexes. Deeply satisfying relationships. Not all men are like your father.'

Chelsea had had enough. He was back to talking about affairs again and it was time he learned that as far as she was concerned that idea was a non-starter.

'If I ever fell in love—which heaven forbid—I'd want the relationship to be permanent,' she snapped, the temper he could so easily make her lose going wildly out of control, making her forget to guard her tongue. 'And, as far as your patronising "all men are not like my father" goes, I know they are. Firstly my father himself, then Tom, Joannie's ex,' she enumerated on her fingers. 'He started playing around with his secretary after Joannie had, quite innocently as it happened, been seen having lunch with an old boyfriend. And then Miles, of course. He made no secret of his extra-marital affairs, and Roger—sex was all he was ever interested in. I don't think the man's been born who can stay faithful to one woman,' she opined heatedly. 'So don't blame me if I choose to steer clear of that kind of emotional mess!'

'Who was Roger?'

The lift of a dark brow, the incisive line of his mouth informed Chelsea that she had been a monumental fool. She'd allowed him to lead her adroitly by the nose, getting her to reveal far more about herself than she had had any intention of doing. And she took a grip of herself and answered airily, 'Someone I once knew. Not important.'

'Important enough to figure in your male rogues' gallery,' he came back quickly, calling her bluff. She shrugged, trying to disguise the fact that her breath was coming far too rapidly.

'I included him as being yet another example of the man who's only interested in one thing.'

'Sex,' Quinn said softly, shaking his head in mock dismay. 'Tch...Tch...' He wasn't quite managing to hide his amusement and Chelsea was twisting her napkin to shreds but she went very still when he asked, with more perception than she had given him credit for, 'You wanted to marry him?'

She had; it had been all she had dreamed of for twelve long months, but she wasn't going to admit that to Quinn. She had been eighteen, just starting college, and, looking back on it, all she knew was that she had been ripe for love. During her childhood she had missed out on the normal affection that came from a happy and stable home life. She had been looking unconsciously for the security of abiding affection, the opportunity to love and be loved in return and Roger had been attending the same college, completing a course in computer studies, and on their second date he had told her he loved her and she, totally gullible, incredibly naïve, had believed him, sure in her ignorance that she, unlike her unfortunate mother, had found a man who could be trusted.

And she had begun to make plans for a wonderful white wedding, for the afterwards with both of them working until they could afford a home, a home for the children they were going to have, children who would grow and develop in the happiness and security she had never had herself. And although Roger had repeatedly asked her to sleep with him she had always refused, telling him that she wanted everything about their future life to be perfect, that their loving would put the seal on the vows which they would eventually make in church. Not understanding his angry frustration because she had felt nothing of that kind herself.

But that hadn't stopped him trying to persuade her and on one never-to-be-forgotten occasion his patience had run out and he had tried to force her, only stopping when her fright and disgust had brought him to his senses. And then he had flung away from her, finally telling her the truth.

He had only said he loved her because that was what he'd thought she wanted to hear, gone along with her when she'd talked of wedding plans because he'd thought she'd be more amenable to sharing his bed. He had never had any intention of marrying her.

'I told you, I don't want to be married,' she skirted the truth now, aware of the stretching and probably revealing silence. Jumping to the attack because that was the best way of defending the walls she'd built around herself, she said laconically, 'When you're through trying to analyse my reasons for remaining celibate, why not admit that you're just as prejudiced? I would be willing to marry if I ever found a man I could love and, probably more importantly, trust. But as that possibility is rather remote I am happy to concentrate on my career. While you're so anti-marriage, it's laughable.'

'But not celibate,' Quinn pointed out, making a painful knot of jealousy lodge under her breastbone as she thought of all the women who had briefly shared his life and his bed. Briefly being the operative word, she reminded herself tartly, ashamed of the reactions he could draw from her.

They had reached the coffee stage and he was leaning back in his chair, very relaxed. And the shadows cast by the low-burning candle made his eyes impossible to read, his whole face controlled, an enigma. Chelsea didn't know what he was thinking until he told her, 'All things considered, we make an ideal couple, the perfect partnership.' He briefly examined the square-cut, perfectly manicured nails of one hand then his gaze drifted slowly up to lock with hers. 'Both wary of permanent emotional commitments, both with good reason. Both wanting each other—wanting until it hurts...'

His eyes were dark with an intensity that made her suck in her breath, and his sensual mouth was set in an uncompromising line as he cut short her hot denial. 'Try to be honest about what you feel, don't let muddled thinking—murky and misguided feelings of shame—colour your judgement. And when you can do that, my pet, we shall be lovers. It's only a matter of time before your direct mind shows you that our loving was meant to happen; it was all settled the moment we met.'

He got to his feet. 'I'm not into making promises because I don't pretend to be clairvoyant, but I do promise you this—we shall be lovers, and for as long as it lasts I will be faithful to you, and only you, because, for better or worse, I am already committed to our future relationship. And I will show you what real fulfilment is. Now——' he extended a hand, his eyes holding hers, refusing to let go '—I shall take you home.'

CHAPTER EIGHT

QUINN did take Chelsea home, just that. Nothing more. She'd been on edge during the journey from the restaurant, sure he would insist on taking her to the penthouse—not that she would have complied, of course—or muscled into her own apartment.

All the way up in the lift she had been tensed up to explosion-point, pysching herself up for the punishing speech she would deliver when he suggested a nightcap, a continuation of the dreadful discussion he'd instigated over the dinner table.

He was arrogantly taking it for granted that they would become lovers and it made her blood boil just to think about it, and she was going to have to make him understand that it simply wasn't going to happen.

She was so wound up that she was shaking all over by the time he delivered her to the door of her apartment. Taking the key from her useless fingers, he opened the door, standing aside for her to precede him, or so she thought, and she turned to tell him to get lost when he dipped his dark head, brushed the lightest of kisses over her lips and walked back to the waiting lift, leaving her standing there, her mouth open with shock.

Tactics, she informed herself nervously as she got ready for bed, taking off her shower cap and pulling a fine cotton nightdress over her head. He had probably planned her seduction with the precision of a military campaign and the next time they met he would go in for the kill.

He wasn't to know that if he had taken her into his arms tonight, kissed her, touched her she would have gone up like a flame. Her treacherous body would have given in without the shadow of a fight.

And a good thing too! she thought, cross with herself. Snatching up a hairbrush, she began to pace the confines of her home, dragging the brush through her long black hair with punishing strokes. The wretch could cut through her careful defences like a hot knife through butter and he had an uncanny knack of reaching the truth—she did want him until it hurt...

Flinging the brush into a corner of the room, she climbed into bed and snapped off the light and lay staring into the darkness, furious with herself. Every time she thought she was well on the way to getting him out of her system he popped up again and demonstrated that the sexual vagaries she had believed herself immune to were alive and kicking. And the very thought of the kind of pressure he would exert when next they met made her go hot and cold with terror.

For meet again they would. She had no doubts about that. She would try to avoid it, of course she would, but going by his past record he would cut through her evasions with no trouble at all. All he had to do was threaten to tell Miles the truth about their engagement. It could be as much as four weeks before the board, with an overriding input from the chairman, would make a final decision about her promotion. Four weeks.

That Quinn wouldn't insist they meet within that space of time was too much to hope for. She pummelled her pillow and the phone by her bed rang out and she knew that her pessimism had been well founded when his deep, sexily husky voice said, 'We shall be attending a charity ball on Saturday evening; wear something glamorous and be ready to leave at nine.'

Chelsea's heart leapt to her throat and began its now well-practised routine of trying to escape from her body. Saturday. Two days away. She couldn't stand it!

'None of your usual objections?' Unforgivable amusement rippled through his velvet voice and she could almost see that infuriating, lazy grin! And she snapped out raggedly, at the end of her tether, 'Would there be any point?'

And he answered, the warmth in his voice curling her bare toes, 'I'm glad you're learning. Are you in bed? What are you wearing?'

'What has that got to do with you?' she demanded, pushing her hair back out of her eyes with a hand that was disgracefully unsteady.

'I'd just like to imagine the way you look, so tell me what you are wearing,' he said unrepentantly, the honey-smooth tones making her temperature rise to danger level, making her lose what little brain power she had left, making her snap out,

'Nothing!' She had meant that her choice of sleeping apparel had nothing to do with him—not that she was naked, but in her agitation she had put it over the wrong way!

And she was thoroughly punished for her unguarded mistake when he murmured, 'That won't tax my imagination, my pet. The image of your naked body has been printed on my retina ever since I saw you in the pool, wearing nothing but a dab of scarlet here and there.' Then he added huskily, his wicked amusement coming unmistakably down the line, 'There couldn't have been more than an inch of fabric all told—and before you slam the phone down in virtuous virginity I'll be away on business until seven on Saturday evening, so I'll arrange for a messenger to deliver the ring at four in the afternoon.'

'What ring?' she demanded tightly, her face still burning with the effects of what he had said regarding the borrowed bikini. And how did he know she was a virgin, anyway?

'Our engagement ring, what else? There's——'

'There's no need for that,' she cut in smartly, thankful to be back on safer ground, but he slid in silkily,

'There's every need. Everyone at the ball will have read the announcement and will expect to see one of the company's best stones glittering on your pretty finger. So you'll wear it for me, and you'll look beautiful for me, and you'll smile for me...' His voice was an intoxicating purr and, despite all logic, her body went boneless with yearning, and he whispered, 'Goodnight, my love,' and the line went dead, and she put the receiver back on its rest and buried her face in her pillow.

She wasn't his 'love' and never would be. But oh, how she wished she was!

Incomprehensibly, she felt weepy the next day, which wasn't like her. And she was late for work again because although she'd woken at the usual time she'd kept drifting off into a misty, private world which contained nothing but his words, his smile, the way he looked at her, making her feel special.

Coming back from the studio, where she'd had a mild altercation over the lighting effects for the first take of a shampoo commercial, she viewed the mound of work on her desk with disgust.

It wasn't like her to find her work a drag, to experience such a marked lack of interest in her job. Perhaps, she thought hopefully, she was coming down with something obnoxious. Something serious enough to explain her unprecedented inertia, to give her a completely valid excuse to stay away from the ball.

Opening a script that had been sent up from the copy department, she tried to concentrate, but her thoughts kept wandering away, and she knotted her brow, trying to figure out why Quinn hadn't gone the whole hog and blackmailed her into his bed. After all, he had blackmailed her into doing everything else! Having dinner with him after the Ryder-Gem party, then lunch, then going to Monk's Norton—not to mention last night.

But had she ever really believed he would carry out his threats?

Her face turned fiery red and she pushed the stack of papers aside, burying her head in her hands. No, of course she hadn't. He wasn't the type to go ahead and ruin another person's career out of pique.

She had instinctively known that all along and only now was she forcing herself to be honest enough to admit it. And admitting it meant what? That he had been playing games and despite all her protests she had gone along with them, pretending to be a victim when all the time she knew she wasn't.

And that meant she was a coward. Emotionally and morally. A stupid twenty-six year old virgin who was so afraid of facing up to the needs and desires of her woman's body that she had to pretend to be forced!

He had never forced her into anything. Led her, maybe, but never forced. And painful honesty obliged her to admit that she had been sexually aware of him ever since they had met for the first time in the swimming-pool in the sports complex back at the apartment block. And simply seeing him at the launch party had given her the idea of asking him to pretend to be her fiancé. A Freudian slip if ever she'd seen one!

And her heart had told her that if she'd refused point blank to comply with any one of his many demands he would have given that insouciant smile of his and tried another tack! He would have never ruined her career, her whole future, but she had refused to listen to what her heart had been telling her, preferring, coward that she was, to pretend he was forcing her to do what she wanted to do all along!

She gave an anguished groan and, from behind her, Molly said, 'Are you all right?'

Chelsea had been so swamped by her painful thoughts that she hadn't heard the door open, and she smiled shakily at her secretary and affirmed, 'Yes, I'm fine, thanks.' So much for coming down with something contagious! All she had caught was a severe and agonising case of honesty!

'You're worried about the interview, poor thing!' Molly said with sympathetic concern, putting a pile of unsigned letters down on the desk. 'You shouldn't be. They'd be fools to spend time and effort advertising for

outsiders. You've run this department single-handedly
for months—and put some great stuff through—and
everyone knows it. Even Sir Leonard will come out of
his Victorian fog eventually and see the daylight! So buck
up, do. Shall I fetch you a nice cup of tea?'

'Oh, I'd love one.' Chelsea gave a heartfelt sigh. She
really had to pull herself together. She had completely
forgotten about the preliminary informal meeting with
Sir Leonard and the other directors this afternoon! If
Molly hadn't reminded her she would have sat here agonising until the night cleaners had swept her out!

Quickly, she pulled her work towards her again and
made a determined effort to plough through it. But for
some reason the career she'd been so dedicated to no
longer seemed so all-important.

'Chelsea? It's me, Joannie.'

Chelsea sagged down on the sofa, her fingers relaxing
around the phone. For some reason she had been afraid
the caller was Quinn, letting her know that he wouldn't
be able to get back in time to attend the ball tonight.
Afraid?

'Have you heard from Mum yet?' her sister was asking
and Chelsea enquired quickly,

'Is anything wrong?'

'Not a thing. She called me a couple of weeks ago.
She and Vito are getting married. I'm so happy for her!'
Joannie sounded very relaxed; the last time Chelsea had
spoken to her she'd hardly been able to make out a word
through the sobs. Her divorce had just come through
and she'd been feeling terrible, on her way to spend a
few weeks in France with a distant cousin neither of them

had met more than twice, to try to recover her equilibrium. Well, she had done that, Chelsea noted as Joannie burbled on, 'After all she went through with Dad, all she did for us, she deserves some happiness. All she's ever really wanted is to be settled.'

'She was settled with us, in Stepney,' Chelsea couldn't help pointing out. She was happy for her mother, of course she was, but the way she had left them could still rankle.

'Oh, but it wasn't the same, was it?' Joannie denied. 'I know for a fact that she could have remarried before, but for us. Not many men want to take on a ready-made family, especially if they happen to be adolescent daughters! We frightened them off! And she only left us when we were adult. I'd got a job and you were finishing college and well on the way to becoming an independent career woman. And she never took a penny from the sale of the house.'

'You're quite right,' Chelsea admitted. With hindsight, everything her sister said made sense and tears pricked the back of her eyes as she added, 'I hope she contacts me, then I can wish her all the happiness in the world.'

And Joannie chuckled, 'Of course she will, dolt! She did try to phone you but couldn't get any answer; you must have been away—or been disconnected because you hadn't paid your bill! Anyway...' she paused to catch her breath '...I've got more news. Good news. Tom and I are getting together again.'

'Joannie—do you think that's wise?' Chelsea heard the screech in her voice and shuddered. But after all the misery her sister had gone through...

'What has wisdom got to do with love?' Joannie wanted to know. 'When the divorce came through he was as shattered as I was. It seemed like the end of the world—to both of us. Which has to say something. He came out to France and, well, we decided to try again. It's a question of trusting in the power of love, gritting your teeth and damn well trusting!'

For a long time after her sister had rung off Chelsea sat staring into the middle distance, thinking of Quinn. Joannie had talked about the power of love, of trusting. Trusting one's future happiness to a single man. It made her feel afraid because it was as if the door to her future had swung open, and he had walked in. And he would be with her through all the years, a lost love, lost yet forever in her heart, her mind. Intangible, never real. Or not to her.

Her mind ranged backwards, asking questions. Why had she given in without a real fight? His saying he would tell Robartes the truth had been a joke; he wouldn't have dropped her in it just like that. Had her token resistance, so easily quelled, been merely that—a token? For form's sake? Yes, of course it had. Had she, even then, wanted him to dominate her? Had she already been falling in love with him?

She got to her feet. Time to run her bath, make herself beautiful for him, wear his ring.

She had spent all morning searching for the perfect dress and now it was lying across her bed. The rich pansy-coloured silk fitted sheath with the shoe-string straps and deeply scooped neckline had cost far more than she could sensibly afford but she would wear it for him, and look beautiful for him because she had done the unthinkable and fallen deeply, irrevocably in love.

And the ring had been delivered, just as he had said it would be, by a security messenger, and it had to be the largest, most perfect diamond she had ever seen. And yes, she would wear it for him, not because the sight of it, glittering on her finger, would stop tongues wagging, but because, for a few bright hours, she could pretend that it actually meant something.

And yes, loving him, admitting that she loved him with a woman's body, heart and mind meant that she could go to him, stay with him, be his woman for as long as he wanted her. But was she brave enough to face the pain, the loss and loneliness when everything ended? He had made no promises, except to remain faithful for as long as the affair lasted.

Could that ever be enough? And after knowing him, loving him, could she ever be the same again?

She didn't know. She simply didn't know.

The music was slow and seductive, pulsing heavily through her veins, and there was magic in the way Quinn held her, in the way their bodies moved as one, and there was something in his eyes that she had never noticed before, something warm and kind and loving. Or maybe it had always been there and she hadn't seen it, preferring to be blind.

But she was seeing clearly now, loving him, knowing in the deep, silent recesses of her heart that whatever he wanted of her she had to give. She simply couldn't fight him any more. And tonight, later, she would tell him so.

'When do you think we can slink away from this thrash?' Quinn wanted to know, nuzzling aside the sleek wings of the silky dark hair she had chosen to wear loose around her shoulders tonight.

His lips nipped at the lobe of her ear and her breath caught in her throat but she managed, 'And not sample the buffet? It looks fantastic, and I'm hungry.'

'So am I, my love, so am I.' The deep, sexy purr of his voice left her in no doubt that food, no matter how delicious, was the last thing on his mind, and his arms tightened around her, his hips thrusting against hers, the heat of the contact fusing them together as they moved slowly, swaying together, on the periphery of the ballroom.

It was as much as Chelsea could do to stay upright, need for him weakening her bones and as she leant her head weakly against his broad, black-clad shoulder he heaved a mock sigh.

'Whatever you say, my lovely little glutton, I'm yours to command. Always.'

If only that were true, Chelsea thought on a fleeting sigh as he slowly turned her in the direction of the elegant buffet room, telling her, 'Two bites of whatever takes your fancy, that's all. I've an intimate supper for two planned for later.' Then she stiffened as he took her hand, tucking it into the crook of his arm, holding it there possessively, and added, 'Enough people have seen my mark of ownership on your finger so, duty done, I want you to myself.'

She glanced up at him quickly, unable to hide her feelings, and he met her bleak blue eyes and said sombrely, 'There will be no pressure, you have my word on that. I can wait, my love.'

His golden gaze was direct, very sober, the warm pads of his fingers tightening reassuringly over her captured hand and the tiny coil of tension in her was eased away because her momentary doubts had nothing to do with fear of pressure, and she was able to tell him, 'Excuse me, I must find the washroom. I won't be long.'

And he lifted her hand to his lips, his eyes intent on hers as he commanded against her skin, 'Don't be.'

And she walked away, her heart beating like a drum. She needed a few moments on her own. Just a few because up until now the evening had been perfect. She had committed herself to him in her mind, emotionally and physically, for as long as fate decreed they would be together, and she had begun to see their relationship as something real and solid, a foundation on which something stronger and more permanent could hopefully be built.

But his remark about enough people having seen the mark of their engagement on her finger had hurt more than she had thought possible, a reminder that nothing was as it seemed.

Tonight they had established themselves as a couple in front of the glittering sponsors of one of the most popular charities going—business moguls, cabinet ministers, the cream of London society with a sprinkling of peers of the realm and two minor Royals. And all done to deal the clinging Sandy the blow that would detach her from Quinn's orbit with complete finality.

A timely reminder of his potential for cruelty, she told herself as she walked slowly back to the crowded ballroom, her emotions firmly under control now. Without his streak of cruelty, Quinn would be perfect, and she was able to look truth in the face at last—thanks to him—able to come to terms with the fact that no human being was perfect. Ever.

Everyone had character flaws that had to be lived with and understood, and she was adult enough to handle this because, while she was with him, he would be hers, only hers, hers for a time of loving that might be short. Or might, with the gods on her side, be forever. She was, for the first time since Roger's betrayal, brave enough to trust the power of love. Her love for Quinn.

But reality was never predictable and she had to keep the courage to face the fact that he might, one day, be trying to shake her off. And if and when that day came she would leave with dignity, taking her memories, treasuring them over the empty years.

She would never, unlike the unfortunate Sandy, force him to go to devious lengths to make her see that she was no longer wanted.

Shaking off the cold-fingered touch of sadness, she hovered in the open double doorway to the glittering ballroom, her lips curving in a small secret smile as she recalled how Quinn had mistaken her moment of bleakness as fear of any pressure he might have brought to bear. Tonight, over that intimate supper he'd talked of, she would be completely honest. Tell him that she loved him, that she wanted to be his lover—no strings except the fidelity he had promised her.

A long walk to the buffet-room, easing her way through the groups of beautiful people who weren't actually dancing. Quinn would probably be waiting, ill-concealed impatience on his utterly handsome face, probably clutching a plate with his selection of food for her. One quail egg and a minute square of toast smothered with caviare! He had made it perfectly plain that he had no intention of waiting while she sampled all the goodies on offer!

Her smile broadening, Chelsea brushed the wings of hair back from her flushed cheeks, and debated the best way of getting past a larger than usual knot of people. Round? Or through?

Round, she thought, preparing to squeeze between a formidable, pearl-plastered dowager and the crimson flock-covered wall with an added obstacle of a group of spindle-legged gilded chairs, a polite murmur of apology on her lips.

But before she could make her presence felt, or get a word out, the dowager remarked to her companions, her plummy voice disparaging, 'It's high time Ryder put his foot down. He must know she's only after one thing— little minx! Arriving late, with her usual fast set, making a public spectacle of herself, and him. The trouble is, Sandy knows how to twist him round her little finger, and he simply can't resist her. Just look at her now!'

Heads swivelled, Chelsea's too. Just hearing that name—Sandy—had made her go cold. Her face set and pale, she clung desperately to the hope that the 'Ryder' who was being so disparaged was someone else, not her Quinn at all.

But it was difficult to miss him. The immense room would have to be packed, bodies stacked one on top of the other until they reached the ceiling, and him right at the bottom of the pile, before anyone could overlook a man with his particular masculine magnetism.

And the girl he was with—more wrapped up in than merely with—was unmissable, too. Copper-red hair tumbled tumultuously over creamy, naked shoulders and her voluptuous body seemed to have been poured into the clinging flame-coloured dress she was almost wearing, and her tiny scarlet-tipped hands were firmly on his shoulders, her lovely face smiling beguilingly into his.

And he was more than happy to be beguiled; in fact he was revelling in it, Chelsea thought, fighting the knife-thrust of agonising jealousy as he caught the bewitching beauty up in his arms, his eyes laughing, intent on the gorgeous, copper-framed face.

Chelsea turned, making her legs take her out of here, as far as the foyer of the sumptuous hotel, not knowing whether she was going to survive this. Not caring.

He hadn't told her that Sandy was a fever in his blood. Poor Quinn. His desperate measures to ensure that she backed out of his life must have been born of a knowledge that he found her irresistible. Too irresistible. He had probably felt the marriage trap closing, and his vain attempts to shut her out of his life were the final death throes of his precious bachelor existence.

Sandy was obviously a sticker. Even the pearly dowager had known that Quinn couldn't resist her. And Sandy wasn't going to let a little thing like an engagement deflect her from her course. Sandy was going to get him in the end.

CHAPTER NINE

'DON'T you ever dare walk out on me like that again!' Quinn's face was a mask of stark fury as Chelsea opened the door to his insistent pounding, his big masculine body bristling with it.

'If the desk clerk hadn't remembered you ordering a taxi I'd have had the whole Metropolitan police force out looking for you now!'

'You'd better come in.' Chelsea stood back, her face white. She was trembling inside, like a wounded animal, but he wasn't to know that.

On reaching the sanctuary of her apartment her first instinct had been to bolt the doors, unplug the phone and creep into bed, curling up with her misery. But knowing Quinn, learning to love him, had taught her to face the truth, no matter how unpalatable. And now she was having to learn how to deal with it.

Facing him now was the hardest thing she had ever had to do. And he had arrived much sooner than she had expected, all things considered. He had been so wrapped up in his former lover that she hadn't expected him to notice her absence for several hours. He hadn't given her time to work out what to tell him. Facing up to the truth in the privacy of her own mind was one thing, letting him in on it was quite another.

'So what got into you?' His voice was insistent, hard, his jaw aggressive. 'Can you imagine how worried I was when you just disappeared off the face of the earth?'

Worried? She shook her head involuntarily, not believing that. Worry implied a degree of concern that simply wasn't there. She'd dented his ego when she'd walked away from that ball. Nothing more.

And what was a dented ego when set against the pain of heartbreak?

'Yes, worried, damn you!'

His eyes were burning into hers, he looked as if he would like to shake her until she broke into little pieces and her body was split with burning pain, as if he had done just that, and she knew that the hurt would never heal until he took her in his arms again, kissed her, touched her, loved her, driving every other coherent thought out of her brain.

But that must never happen. Not now. Not ever. Loving him, she would have gone to him gladly, treasuring their time together. But she wouldn't be a substitute for Sandy, she wouldn't be used as a shield to protect him against the other woman's fatal fascination. One look at the two of them together had told her that, however much he might try to fight it, Sandy was in his blood. He would go whenever she called.

Chelsea knew she couldn't live on that kind of knife-edge, always watching for signs, wondering when the glamorous redhead would walk back into his life and take him away.

'Have you nothing to say?' Quinn's voice was cold and crisp now, his jagged rage under control, but his fists were bunched into the pockets of his immaculate narrow black trousers and a tiny muscle jerked revealingly at the side of his tight jaw.

'I'm sorry,' Chelsea got out breathlessly, biting down hard on the corner of her lower lip until she tasted blood. She had never seen him this angry before, not even when he'd stalked out of Monk's Norton after she'd called a halt to his lovemaking.

'Is that all?' The look he flicked over her was iced with contempt and she instinctively backed away, crossing her arms over her breast, wishing she'd had time to change into old jeans and a shirt. She felt like bursting into tears, sobbing her heart out for what she had almost had, what she had lost.

Then anger took over, cold and analytical. She had been seduced from her life of calm unemotionalism, seduced into believing that, for her, love could be enough, that, whatever his faults, his dislike of long-term commitments, she loved him with a breadth and depth that transcended everything she had dreamed possible.

It had been he who had placed the burden of truth on her shoulders, and she who had to carry it. She had been willing to share her life with him into the foreseeable future, believing him when he'd said he would keep faith. But seeing how he'd reacted to the irresistible wiles of the woman he was desperately trying to fend off had opened her eyes to another truth.

'Sorry!' he derided, the sudden glitter of his eyes making her heartbeat quicken.

He took a couple of steps towards her, and she knew his intention as if he had shouted it aloud in words of one syllable, and she said 'Don't!', her voice coming thickly, and one arched black brow curved up in satanic mockery as he moved even closer, crowding her.

Shaking, she teetered back, felt the edge of the coffee-table against her calves and didn't know whether she would have fallen or not because his arms went round her, hauling her against the hard warmth of his body, his hands splayed out against the burning skin of her back, revealed by the seductive dress she had not had time to change out of.

Trembling fiercely with her attempts to control the desire to simply melt against his masculine strength, she put her fists up, trying to fend him off, but his head swooped down, his mouth punishing her with a kiss that expunged every coherent thought from her mind. And her fists opened, like flowers blossoming languidly in the light, just as her lips opened beneath his, and he moved his body against her, his heated arousal setting in train a series of sensual shock waves that had her melting helplessly against him.

He had brought the battle right to her and she was giving in without a fight, her defences shattered as they always were with him.

No longer inviolate, Chelsea gave a tiny smothered moan as his lips gentled hers and finally left them to trail devastating sensation down the pure line of her throat. And her fingers slid up to touch his face, tightening there as his lips found what they'd so determinedly sought—the deep cleft between her throbbing breasts.

His mouth was hot, burning her up, and she shuddered with irrepressible desire, hardly aware of what he was doing as his hands slid the narrow straps off her silky shoulders then moved oh, so slowly downwards, learning the blossoming shape of her, cradling her naked breasts, dropping light, suckling, tantalising kisses on first one straining peak and then the other.

Chelsea closed her eyes, her head flung back, the excitement making her dizzy, her body boneless, her will totally subjugated beneath the heady mastery of Quinn's sexual domination. She needed this intimacy, needed him. He was a drug in her bloodstream, he was love in her heart, he was the mate in her soul.

The slight metallic whisper of the zip, the rustle of silky fabric as her dress fell around her feet, the ragged hiss of his suddenly indrawn breath as his hands cupped her shoulders, holding her slightly away from him as his brooding eyes devoured her almost naked body had her crying out with the intense shock of her aching desire for him. And then he lifted his eyes slowly, finding and holding hers, and there was triumph there, that and something else as he said hoarsely, 'You want me as much as I want you.' And then his voice gentled and there was a smile in it somewhere, just a hint of the potent, unforgettable charm which he could call up at will.

His hold on her was easy now, relaxed, as if he knew he had her captive by so much more than force, and, held by his potent spell, she lifted her hands again to his face, her fingertips soft with tender, aching wonder, learning the hard, beloved contours, her eyes held by his magnetic golden gaze.

'Don't ever run from me again, my love,' he commanded huskily, his eyes dropping now to the full pout of her bruised mouth. 'What we have is too damned beautiful to waste.'

Helplessly, she believed him. How could she not when every atom of her being ached and trembled with her love for him, her need, the need that transcended every self-protective, logical thought she had ever had?

She was lost, and he knew it, hopelessly lost in the dark spell of his enchantment, and when he scooped her up into his arms her own curved mindlessly around his neck, her head nuzzling into the hard breadth of his shoulders and she was where she was meant to be.

'You belong with me, you don't need to fight it any more,' he said huskily, echoing her hazy thoughts, putting them more concisely than she had been able to manage.

Perhaps, unconsciously, she had been looking for a man such as he all her adult life. Looking for love, for a passion that made all else pale into insignificance, never believing she would find it. But every muzzy thought vanished from her brain when he dipped his head to kiss her bare shoulder, exquisite, teasing, delicious kisses that covered the burning, soft satin skin, making her drown in a sensual whirlpool of his creating.

He was carrying her to her bedroom and as he nudged the door open with his knee she couldn't even manage the smallest protest. She didn't want to. She loved him so much that it hurt, an aching need that only he could assuage. And he placed her almost reverently on her little white virginal bed, dropping her demure cotton night-dress on to the floor, and she heard his sudden intake of breath, saw the fevered glitter of his eyes as he leant forward, removing the last, lacy scrap of covering, pulling the tiny briefs gently down the length of her slender legs.

'You are utterly, utterly beautiful.' His smoky voice was raw with need and then he was on the bed with her, his arms crushing her unresistant body to the savage length of his, kissing her—her lips, her eyes, her neck, trailing along the fragile span of her collarbone, lingering, before moving inexorably down to the aching fullness of her breasts, tasting every inch of her body with an urgency that made her burn with desire, made her cry out her need, the whimpered plea a counterpoint to his ragged breathing.

The ecstasy was a wildness in her, a wildness she hadn't known existed, something that demanded total and utter surrender, a surrender that was inevitable and oh, so right.

And something wild and desperate had her reaching out for him as he withdrew, holding on to him as if she could never let him go, and he caught both her hands in both of his, his voice taut with desire as he told her, 'I know, I know.' Slowly, he turned her hands, his golden eyes glittering briefly into hers before he placed lingering kisses into her curled palms, his tongue smooth and moist and warm in the exact centre of each.

And then he lifted his head and the skin was pulled tight over the bones of his face and his voice was a husky promise as he murmured, 'I'm going to take you, and take you slowly. I'm going to make it as good for you as I know how. And to do that——' his long mouth curved in a wicked smile '—I'm going to have to slow down the pace. You've brought me to the edge of control, like a randy teenager.' Carefully, he disengaged his hands from hers, removing his tie, unbuttoning his shirt before he shrugged out of his jacket. And Chelsea felt unbelievable pressure spiral up inside her and she had to touch him, caress him . . .

Hungrily, she slid her hands beneath his shirt, her fingertips, her eager palms, learning the shape, the strength, the warmth and power of him, feathering up to the strong column of his neck, touching his face, the abrasive toughness of his jaw, unable to get enough of him.

And her questing hands had reached the thick darkness of his hair and, deep in its sable depths, the diamond glittered coldly, suddenly, its many facets reflecting ice, the underlying coldness of the way he saw their relationship, reminding her with a painful, devastatingly sudden clarity of the way he was using her.

She flinched, as if she had received a knife-thrust to her heart, and then her body went very cold, very still, her mind completely clear now, pain eating at the edges, making her want to cry.

As far as Quinn was concerned, she was simply a woman to use as a shield against the danger that Sandy represented. The danger that he might, against his will, find the gorgeous redhead irresistible enough to marry, the danger that he might spend the rest of his life wondering if she had married him for his money.

The fact that he found her, Chelsea, fanciable enough to take into his bed would, in his opinion, be one big bonus. But it wasn't enough for her, and never could be. She had been prepared to fight for his love, for the hope that what they had would grow into a deeper, more permanent and worthwhile emotion for him. But she couldn't fight Sandy's fatal fascination.

Slowly, she brought her hands down, crossing them over her exposed breasts. There was little she could do, with any dignity, to cover the rest of her, the slenderness that had been so wantonly yet naturally displayed for his delight.

And she told him tiredly, her heart a dying, heavy thing deep within her aching, unfulfilled body, 'I can't, Quinn. I know what you want but it's not enough for me. For me it has to be all or nothing.'

Fidelity, faithfulness, for as long as their relationship lasted, would have been all she could have the right to ask. But even that small comfort would have been denied her. All Sandy had to do was put in an appearance and Quinn was caught in her spell. From the disparaging remarks she had overheard, everyone knew he couldn't resist her.

The elaborate engagement charade he'd put up as protection was no protection at all. And he knew it and, typically, was fighting as hard as he knew how. But she wasn't going to be his weapon. She had too much pride and self-respect to allow herself to be used that way.

For long moments his golden eyes scanned her pale face, the soft wings of dark hair adding a vulnerable dimension which was at odds with the compressed line of her mouth, and he said slowly, as if her bald statement, her unequivocable withdrawal were something he was at last coming to terms with,

'And that's your final word. You're willing to throw away what you know we have—could have—together, all for an outdated principle.' His mouth twisted. 'You're no better than the rest. Hot on promises, cold on delivery.'

He stood up with a jerk, reaching for his jacket.

'I know the way the female mind works—bring a man to the edge of his control and then hold out for marriage. Sorry to disappoint you, my dear, but I'm not about to beg you to name the day.' He gave her a last, bitter look before striding to the door, then he turned to her, his face bleak, prolonging the silence until Chelsea felt she would explode into wild, screaming hysteria.

Then he told her bitterly, his features almost brutal, making it impossible for her to believe in the existence of all the devilish charm she had come to know so well, 'If you're afraid to trust, you're afraid to live. And cowardice makes a cold bedfellow, my dear. Think about it.'

Think about it. She thought of little else as she lay in the darkness, wide-eyed, dry-eyed. She wasn't going to weep, because what had happened had been a lucky escape. If she had allowed him to become her lover then she would have been lost forever. She would have agreed to live with him and she would have lived with love and hope. Love for him, hope that eventually he would grow to love her in return, love her enough to make their relationship permanent.

But there would have been no hope. What she had overheard and seen with her own eyes had convinced her of that, and love would have turned to pain, and pain to bitterness . . .

So no, she wasn't going to weep . . .

And morning took ten years to come and she greeted the new day with no enthusiasm but loads of determination. Somehow, some way, she would get back to being how she was, sure of herself, of the choice she had made for her life, ready to push her career along for as far as it would go. She would keep all her emotions for her work. She had done it before and could do it again.

The interlude with Quinn was over. The fantasy finished. Or almost.

Checking her reflection in the mirror before setting out for the agency, she approved the image. Neat clerical-grey suit with a faint pinstripe worn over a soft blue blouse that saved the ensemble from total severity. Black hair caught back in her nape with a plain tortoiseshell clip, make-up slightly heavier than normal—a necessity, really, to hide the dark, haunted rings beneath her eyes.

One more thing to do before the whole sorry chapter could end. Return his ring.

She should have done it last night, of course, and thus avoided having to confront him again, she thought worriedly as the lift soared towards the penthouse suite. Quite simply, she hadn't thought of it. Her thoughts had been preoccupied with the truth of Quinn's pitiful attempts at resisting the irresistible.

The very idea of describing anything about Quinn Ryder as pitiful gave her pause for thought. And she stood in the very centre of the carpeted foyer at the entrance to the penthouse suite, her deep blue eyes anguished, her mind reeling with half-formed thoughts. And when she at last began to make some sense of the messages that were battling around in her brain she dragged in a deep breath and squared her shoulders.

He was losing his battle to keep the delectable redhead out of his life and maybe, loving him, caring about him, she should have offered to help. Not by becoming his live-in lady, that was for sure; there was only so much punishment she could take and her instincts for self-preservation had had her smartly backing out of any such arrangement.

But she could surely talk to him seriously, she reflected, straightening her spine. She could tell him she knew the truth—that he was willing to go to any lengths to keep the woman who was determined to become part of his life very firmly out of it. She could point out that if he found her so difficult to resist then he maybe should give up and admit he needed her on a permanent basis.

It would be the hardest thing she had ever had to do; she knew that as soon as the tears she had refused to shed last night pricked painfully at the back of her eyes. But, because she loved him, she would do it. Besides, she owed it to herself to make him understand that she hadn't backed off last night because she'd been planning to make him want her enough to offer marriage.

Pressing the buzzer before her nerve failed her completely, she wondered at the well of compassion he had so unexpectedly tapped within her, how loving him made her want to help him, made her selfless.

Though she didn't deserve a medal, she thought wryly, trying to hold on to her precarious composure as she waited for him to open the door.

After all, she wasn't sacrificing anything, was she? There had never really been any long-term hope for her, had there? True, he had fancied her enough to want to be her lover. Having another woman might have taken his mind off Sandy for a time. But it hadn't worked out quite like that, had it? The moment the other woman had put in an appearance at the ball last night he had been all over her. He hadn't been able to help himself.

The moment the door began to open Chelsea's heart jumped like a landed fish and the ring she had been clutching in the palm of her hand bit painfully into her flesh. It was going to be difficult to hide her feelings, to point him in the direction of another woman when she wanted him so much herself.

Her hazily prepared opener emptied out of her brain and her throat closed tightly, painfully, because she wasn't looking into Quinn's darkly compelling features but into a pair of sleepy brown eyes set in a piquantly lovely face—the whole framed in a rumpled mass of copper hair.

Sandy was wearing what had to be one of Quinn's shirts and nothing else. One scarlet-tipped hand kept the edges of the fabric together, the other went up to hide a tiny, cat-like yawn.

Woken from her haven in Quinn's arms, she looked much younger than she had done last night in the flame-coloured dress and Chelsea knew she was going to pass out on the spot, she just knew it! Fighting the sensation of nausea that was rolling around in the pit of her stomach, she held out her hand, disclosing the fabulous diamond set in its platinum band and managed tightly, 'See Quinn gets this, please.' And she walked away, praying that her legs would hold her upright until she reached the sterile cocoon of the lift.

Once there, leaning weakly against the satin-finished steel, she fought back tears, furious with herself.

Who had she been trying to fool? All those airy-fairy, priggish notions about selflessly pointing him in Sandy's direction had been nothing more than hogwash. She'd been piously lying to herself. Mentally patting herself on the back for being so damned noble! When all the time she had been hoping that he would have denied wanting Sandy at all, that he would have protested that the only woman he wanted in his life, found remotely irresistible, was herself—Chelsea Stupid Viner!

CHAPTER TEN

'THAT was just what I needed,' Joannie sighed, forking up the last morsel of the lasagne and salad that Chelsea had prepared when they'd arrived back at the apartment. 'Weddings always make me weepy—Mum looked fantastic, didn't she? And Vito so adoring. I'm glad they decided to marry in London but I wish they'd stayed on for just a few days, instead of flying back to Rome straight off like that.'

'I expect Vito wanted to celebrate with his family at the Italian end,' Chelsea put in, absently fingering the fine gold chain which Vito had presented her with at the small lunch party following the civil ceremony.

She had altered her opinion of her mother's relationship with the rotund Italian; they obviously thought the world of one another. She was happy for them. But Joannie was mourning.

'I still wish they'd hung around a bit longer—what with Tom having to leave straight after the ceremony to attend that wrap-up interview in Shrewsbury. Mind you——' she began stacking the used plates '—it does mean promotion and a useful salary boost, and we'll like living in the sticks. Much better for raising a family.' She turned a pretty shade of pink and carted the dishes out to the small, functional kitchen. Chelsea followed, plugged in the coffee-maker, and Joannie grinned.

157

'We'll have a big family party when Tom and I re-marry, but we can't set the date until we've found a house up there—he's promised to bring back a whole bunch of estate agent's particulars, and it shouldn't take too long to pick out something suitable. Are you sure you don't mind my staying here with you for the next week or two?'

She was vigorously clattering dishes in the sink and Chelsea grabbed a tea-towel and told her, 'Of course not, lovey. The sofa turns itself into a bed, though I can't vouch for its comfort.'

She could understand why her sister didn't want to go back to the dismal bed-sit she'd occupied since the break-up of her marriage; it held bad memories of a trau-matically miserable and lonely time. And as Tom would be staying with an old schoolfriend in Clerkenwell until he took up his new job in Shrewsbury it made sense for Joannie to stay here until the couple set up a new home. But she did add warningly, 'I've put the apartment up for sale; I've already had one firm offer.'

'You've what?' Joannie's mouth fell open. 'But I thought you were really happy here! The place is stylish and quiet—perfect for you—and so handy for that precious job of yours.'

She was staring as if she couldn't believe what she'd heard and Chelsea wiped the last of the dishes and began pouring coffee, her face set.

She'd been so proud of her apartment; it had been a symbol of her achievement, her success in her chosen career. But she knew she couldn't stay on here, not with Quinn—and, very probably, Sandy—occupying the penthouse suite. She simply couldn't. And when they weren't here they would be at Monk's Norton, and she would know it because he went to his lovely country house just as often as he could. And she couldn't bear knowing they were there, married, bringing up their children—Quinn's children—— Oh, dear God, she couldn't think of small, dark-haired, golden-eyed replicas of the man she loved without wanting to throw back her head and howl!

'And where will you go—have you found another pad yet?' Joannie wanted to know, and Chelsea shook her head, not trusting herself to speak, and began carrying the coffee through to the sitting-room, the cups rattling on their saucers because she just couldn't keep her hands steady.

She had no idea where she would go. The idea of alternative living accommodation simply hadn't entered her head because the pressure to get away from Quinn's orbit hadn't left room for anything else. There hadn't even been room for her job and something of what she was going through must have shown on her face because Joannie took the cups from her, put them on the coffee-table and said, 'Tell me what's wrong, Sis,' and put loving arms around her in the way they'd tried to comfort each other when they'd been very young and things had been bad at home. 'It's a man, isn't it?' she decided, her voice compassionate, and Chelsea burst into messy tears because she and Joannie had always been close, clinging to each other when their childhood world had seemed to be falling apart, and she couldn't keep her misery to herself a moment longer.

And when her sobs had quietened down to the hiccuping stage she related the whole sorry tale between sips of cooling coffee, and Joannie poured the last of the bottle of wine they'd shared with their meal, put it into her sister's hands and demanded, 'Are you sure you've got the right end of the stick? From what you've told me, he seemed dead keen.' She curled her legs under her on the sofa, opposite Chelsea. 'Drink your wine and try to think. Use that brain you've always been so proud of. Now, try this on for size—he's mad about you, and you turned him down, so he consoled himself with the redheaded harpy.'

'No way.' Chelsea shook her head. 'You didn't see them together at that ball, or hear what I heard. From what the pearly queen said, everyone—but everyone—knows he can't keep his hands off her. And he told me himself——' she wrinkled her brow, trying to recall his exact words '—that he was glad to pretend to be engaged because it would get rid of Sandy once and for all. His actual words were, "I've had a particularly persistent female on my back for months. If she—Sandy—thinks I'm madly in love and about to be married she'll finally get the message and move out of my life." He then went on to say that, in his experience, women only wanted marriage as a passport to financial security for life.'

She swirled the remains of the wine round in her glass and Joannie uncurled her legs and went to open another bottle, filling Chelsea's glass to the brim, and Chelsea gulped at it gratefully. It was dulling the pain, just a little. She could now understand why some people drank to drown their sorrows!

And she told her sister solemnly, feeling so sorry for Quinn that her eyes filled with tears again, 'He's crazy in love with Sandy, but he hasn't been able to admit it. Well, he must have admitted it on the night of the ball, after he'd left me. He must have called her, proposed to her, and she would have gone to his place like a shot and—er—sealed the bargain. And even though the poor love's given in at last he'll spend the rest of his life wondering if Sandy married him for his money. He's got this cynical bee in his bonnet, and he can't get rid of it.'

'Poor love!' Joannie scoffed. 'He sounds like a regular bastard to me!'

'No.' Chelsea shook her head. She couldn't explain why she felt so much compassion for the man who had turned her life upside-down, emptied it out and left her with nothing but a pain where other people kept their hearts.

She had started out distrusting the whole male population, but, at least, she had learned. From Joannie, from Mum, from Quinn himself, and one day—not yet, of course, but one day—she might find herself marrying a man because she liked and respected him, settling for companionship, the pleasure of sharing a life, the ups and the downs. Maybe having children. Maybe. She couldn't think that far ahead. Not yet.

'Have you seen anything of him since that night?' Joannie asked, her eyebrows rising to her hairline as her hitherto abstemious sister sloshed more wine into her glass.

Chelsea said quickly, to disguise the pain, 'No. He'll have written me off completely. After all, even if he hadn't got as far as proposing to Sandy, and she'd changed her mind about holding out for marriage and shared his bed because she couldn't help herself, I returned his ring through her, so she'll know the field's clear again.' She didn't know if she was making much sense—she no longer seemed to have the ability to think very clearly—but, observing the puzzled frown on Joannie's face, she went back to the original question and elaborated, 'I did see him once, as he was getting into the lift, and another time driving away from the car park. He didn't see me. If he'd wanted to, he knew where I lived.'

And that hurt more than she could say. It had been two weeks now since he'd walked away from her, telling her that cowardice would make a cold bedfellow, and she'd expected him to return, to pour more scorn down on her head, to berate her for returning his ring through Sandy, to tell her, even, that the redhead had changed his mind about marriage at last. Anything.

But there had been nothing. Nothing at all, and she had felt lonelier and more unhappy than she could ever remember, only one thing on her mind—the desperate need to get rid of her apartment and move as far away from him as she could reasonably get.

She thoroughly deserved the pounding headache, she thought disgustedly, rummaging through one of the drawers in her desk for the bottle of aspirin tablets she knew she had somewhere. She would take a couple when Molly came with her morning coffee and hope she could get through the rest of the day. Never again would she demolish the best part of a whole bottle of wine!

Joannie had already left for her job as a secretary with an insurance company when Chelsea had crawled out of her bed this morning. The sofa had been returned to its regular use, the spare duvet folded neatly at one end, a note in her sister's handwriting left on the coffee-table, informing her that she would not be in until late that evening as she'd be meeting Tom's train at Euston, having dinner with him at their favourite restaurant and poring over estate agents' particulars.

Everyone seemed to be happy, getting their lives together, Chelsea thought on a wave of self-pity. Joannie and Tom, and Mum and Vito. And she was happy for them; of course she was. And one day she would be happy for herself, she vowed staunchly, pulling a pile of paperwork towards her and trying to ignore the hammers that were thumping the inside of her skull.

And when Molly came in with her coffee she swallowed the aspirin tablets and closed her aching eyes briefly, thankful that her usually observant and forthright secretary hadn't commented on her pallor, the red-rimmed eyes that were a legacy of her weeping bout the evening before, the haggard look that was down to unprecedented alcoholic over-indulgence.

She hadn't finished her coffee and the tablets hadn't begun to work when Molly burst back in, her air of suppressed excitement making her look as if she were about to explode.

'You've to go to the chairman's office at once,' she imparted on a breathless gabble. 'All those rumours— dead right—as if you didn't know! You might have let on!' Then she tilted her head consideringly, grinning, 'I'll forgive you. It wouldn't have been ethical, would it? Anyway, he's waiting, so you'd better get a move on. It's bound to be confirmation of your promotion.'

Chelsea sighed and got to her feet, regretting the peaceful ten minutes that might have seen the back of a headache which was getting more ferocious by the second. She hadn't given her promotion a single thought for the last two weeks. It had no longer seemed important. And she hadn't paid any attention to the rumours that had been flying around, the air of tension that had gripped the staff at the agency.

She had done her job to the best of her ability because she was paid handsomely to do just that, but her heart hadn't been in it. Her heart had been . . .

Well, she wasn't going to think about that, about Quinn. From this moment on she was going to put him firmly out of her mind. Senseless to yearn over what might have been, to mourn what was. Senseless.

Padding along the thickly carpeted corridor towards Sir Leonard's office, past the boardroom, she made a conscious effort to erase the tiny frown-lines from between her red-rimmed eyes. She was no longer sure about that coveted promotion. She was moving out of her apartment and the idea suddenly came to her that she might as well move out of London. The city was a lonely place and with Joannie and Tom moving to the country it would be even lonelier. She had never minded being alone before, but loving Quinn had made her vulnerable.

Shoving that thought aside with characteristic determination, she took a few moments to compose herself before knocking on the great man's door. If he offered her the job, she would take it, and work something out from there. Official confirmation of her ability to run a high-tech, high-powered job on her own would look good on her CV if she did decide, eventually, to move to a provincial agency or explore the possibilities of working on a regional TV station.

Sir Leonard's secretary, who always reminded Chelsea of an elderly piranha, looked up from her obsessively tidy desk in the outer office, bestowed an amazingly sweet smile and instructed, 'Walk right in, he is expecting you.'

And Chelsea did as she'd been bidden, marvelling. She had never seen Miss Natch smile, and neither, to her knowledge, had anyone else! So it must be promotion, she decided, opening the door to Sir Leonard's office after a courteous tap. If she ever raked up enough courage, she would advise Miss Natch to smile more often. It did wonders for her. And then the half-smile that had been flirting with the corners of her mouth fled, her face turning to stone. Turning red. Then white. Deathly white as her headache increased a thousandfold and her legs turned to water.

Quinn!

Afterwards, she would never recall whether she had spoken his name aloud or whether it had merely rattled around inside her head like a recurring dream. But she heard him say, 'Sit down. You look like a punch-drunk flyweight,' indicating a chair on the opposite side of the huge mahogany desk.

So she did. The only other choice was to collapse in a heap on the floor, because seeing him again, seeing him here, not knowing why but guessing, had knocked the stuffing out of her, left her like a gutted rag doll. And as she took a few seconds to compose herself, looking down on her hands knotted together in her grey-skirted lap, she wished she'd taken notice of the rumours regarding some unspecified but huge change that had been flying around. And when she lifted her eyes to encounter his steady yellow gaze, his perfectly expressionless features, he confirmed what she already thought she knew.

'As of today, Ryder-Gem controls Triple A. I made Sir Leonard an offer he couldn't refuse. And from this moment on you answer solely to me. Understood?'

She did. Only too well. So why had he sent for her? Why here, why now? He could have contacted her a hundred times during the last two weeks. Why leave it until now?

Unless... Taking a very deep breath, she injected some sense into her brain. He didn't want to know her on a social level, not any more, not after what had happened. But, having acquired the agency, he would have to deal with her on a business footing. Hence the summons to his office. And she adopted what she hoped was a brightly intelligent expression and surmised, 'Then the rumours must have been right; you were dissatisfied with the way your own people were handling the Ryder-Gem advertising and, instead of looking for an independent agency, you decided to buy one up, one with a proven track record. That way you could have complete control over the Ryder-Gem campaigns, take precedence over all the other clients.'

That must be the answer, of course. And she was pleased with her sagacity, the way she was handling this, outwardly in control and reasonably serene even though she was nearly going out of her mind as she contemplated having to work for him and with him into the foreseeable future.

But that was before he answered with chilling smoothness, 'If that's the way you prefer to look at it for now, then go ahead. However, I have to warn you that my motives weren't quite that straightforward.'

'No?' The single word came out on a whisper, her eyes winging up to his, slanting blue eyes, bruised with pain, dark with the knowledge of how much she, fool that she was, loved this man.

Slowly, she moistened her lips which had suddenly gone dry as a desert, and watched him watch her, saw his eyes darken as they followed the tell-tale movement of her pointed pink tongue.

'No.' The affirmation was cool and he was leaning back now, his elbows on the arms of his chair, his hands steepled in front of his mouth, hiding his expression. 'I want you,' he said with slow deliberation. 'I want you to have what you want. Everything. All it takes.' His half-hooded eyes brooded into hers, as if evaluating her understanding and reception of what he had said, and Chelsea's heart stopped, stopped for long, agonising seconds, then pounded on, pushing her blood through her veins as he continued levelly, 'Providing certain conditions are met, you are, as of this moment, head of the TV commercials department. With a seat on the board to follow. Further and rapid promotion. Robartes will go, eventually. I don't intend to employ a man who would stoop to blackmail; therefore——'

The rush of blood to her head had Chelsea on her feet. Trembling. She couldn't control the way her body shook with outrage, disgust and the shame of loving a man who would do this to her. And she couldn't control her tongue, either, and she spat out, 'You're a great one to talk! You've done nothing but blackmail me, force me to do as you wanted, ever since we met! Miles Robartes is an angel compared to you! And I will not, not,' she repeated vehemently, stamping her foot, making the hammers inside her head go into overdrive, 'be your mistress!'

'I will never ask you to be my mistress again.' His voice was as cool as the eyes that were fixed on her furious face, and she wasn't going to swallow that, not for a moment. Hadn't he just stated that her promotion depended upon her meeting 'certain conditions'? She knew, to her cost, the conditions that Quinn Ryder dealt out! He must still, pathetically, be trying to fend off Sandy. Well, he would just have to find some other female to do his dirty work!

And she tacked on nastily, hating him, 'Then what was it you had in mind? A one-night stand?' She shot him a withering look and turned on her heels, stamping to the door, and, when she was halfway through it, swung around, delivering her parting shot, her final word. 'Please accept my resignation. I will stay on for exactly as long as it takes to type it out formally.'

And how she regained the privacy of her office, she never knew, and it took several attempts before she could get her resignation typed out minus glaring errors. Sealing it into an envelope, addressing it to him, she stalked into the outer office and slapped it down in front of the startled Molly, then stalked right back and began emptying her desk.

She'd had it with Quinn. Had it! He had no consideration for her feelings, none whatsoever. He didn't care what he put her through as long as he got his own way.

Well, he could go and jump off a high cliff with lead weights on his feet, for all she cared. Or he could spend the rest of his life being hounded by redheaded harpies—and serve him right!

Her head high, her spine rigid, Chelsea walked out of Triple A for the very last time, her bits and pieces in a plastic carrier requisitioned from the bewildered Molly. And she was stepping into the lift which would take her to her home when someone walked in right behind her, and the hackles rose on the back of her neck because she knew, even without turning, exactly who it was.

And he said, his voice clipped with anger, 'I warned you about ever daring to run out on me again.' And that was a threat, if ever she'd heard one, and she turned, slowly and reluctantly; he was leaning back against one of the walls, his arms crossed over his broad, grey-suited chest, black brows lowered over fuming yellow eyes.

Anger was still riding her, making her reckless, and she flung back furiously, 'So what are you going to do about it? Turn me over your knees and beat me?'

'Don't tempt me!' Tanned skin was drawn tight over his cheekbones, the sensuality of his beautiful mouth masked by a tight-lipped impatience that should have warned her not to play with this particular fire.

But she was past caring; he had hurt and disgusted her too much, and she shot straight back, her eyes like glittering sapphire ice, 'Bullies don't frighten me, so you can take your macho ego and put it where it hurts! And while we're on the subject of bullies—you don't blackmail me again. Ever!'

The look of stark brutality which darkened his memorable features put the lie to her earlier proud statement and, thankfully, the lift stopped at her floor and she scampered out with more haste than dignity and her heart performed a series of painful acrobatics as he exited with her, catching her elbow in one inescapable hand, swinging her round so that her purloined carrier flew out of her hand, spilling the pathetic debris of her working life over the soft, dove-grey carpeting.

'Oh!' Her protest was squeaked into utter silence, her mouth a rosy circle of dismay so complete that she didn't, for the moment, know what to do about it.

Quinn was still holding her, his grip on her arm merciless, and his body was merely inches away from hers and, despite the frozen mask of his face, she could judge the pace of his heartbeat from the rapid rise and fall of his magnificent chest. A pace that matched the heavy pounding beneath her own breasts.

This close, he was dangerous. He should be locked in a cage, separated from the female members of the public by iron bars! She gulped nervously, trying to drag herself together, fighting the instinct to dissolve into tears of helpless femininity and hurl herself against that oh, so tempting chest. But he had made a fool of her once too often, hadn't he? And it wasn't going to happen again, was it?

Summoning every last scrap of her courage, Chelsea glared back into his eyes and pronounced witheringly, 'If you want a woman to help you get rid of Sandy, then you're going to have to look elsewhere. I'm through being coerced into playing your sick games.' She drew a snorting breath through her nostrils, getting into her stride, ignoring the look of blank amazement that widened his eyes, creased his brow.

It was past time for him to hear a few home-truths, and she would be the one to do it. He had made her suffer enough, after all.

'You once called me a coward—and perhaps with some justification—but you're the biggest coward of all!' Her tirade faltered momentarily as his features softened perceptibly, then she shook her head and snipped on, 'If you're not man enough to admit you want Sandy permanently in your life, or big enough, strong enough, to admit you'll never get rid of all that cynicism you tote around and tell her, finally, that she's wasting her time if she expects you to accept the commitment of marriage—tell her to get lost, if you like—then I'm sorry for you!

His grip on her arm had relaxed considerably. His wretched thumb was actually sliding sensually up and down her sleeve, heating the flesh beneath the thin fabric, and the devil was smiling, damn him! Trying to blind her with that incredible, lazy smile, the smile that had once made her go weak at the knees.

But he wasn't going to use that charm on her ever again. The hurt he had inflicted was unforgettable. But she wasn't going to think of that, not just now. She was going to hang on to her justifiable anger, see if she wasn't! It was the one thing that could get her through these final moments with him.

Releasing her arm from his grasp wasn't nearly as difficult as she had feared it might be, but her knees were shaking as she turned away and knelt to gather up the shameful bits and pieces that had resided in the drawer back at her office.

Tights in unopened packets, tights discarded because of ladders—and forgotten about, because she'd been too busy, too involved in her work to think about such inconsequentialities. Odds and ends of make-up, tissues, a sticky paper bag which split as she touched it and revealed a nibbled-at doughnut.

Oh, why hadn't she hurled the whole horrible muddle into her waste-basket, sorted it out back at her office instead of bundling it all into a bag and stalking out?

And Quinn, drat him, was kneeling too. And she could sense him grinning. Helping her—huh! As he reached for a nearly empty bottle of cologne, she pushed at his large capable hand, hissing furiously, 'Go away! Just leave me alone, will you?' He had ruined her life, made her love him when she hadn't wanted to, made her resign from her job, forced her to put her home on the market. What more did he want? Blood?

And he told her exactly what more he wanted as he unhurriedly shovelled the last of the shaming debris into the carrier.

'There's someone I want you to meet.' And as she opened her mouth on a swift refusal to do any such thing he stalled her smoothly, his voice containing a sharp edge of steel behind the warm velvet patina. 'And just for once you will do exactly as you're told *without*,' he stressed in a tone that would have made a strong man cringe, 'shouting the odds in your usual uncompromising fashion.'

Not waiting to hear if she was about to shout the odds, or anything else, he bundled her resisting body over to the door to the stairwell, not waiting for the lift. Chelsea was digging her heels in, clutching the despised carrier to her heaving chest as he flung open the door. Then, giving her an exasperated glance which was tinged, she noted suspiciously, with laughter, he scooped her up into his arms and took the stairs to the penthouse suite two at a time.

And he didn't let go of her until he'd carried her through to the fabulous sitting-room, then, not even breathing hard now, he slid her down the length of his body until her feet were touching the floor.

She didn't trust his mood, didn't trust anything about him, and the floor seemed to be heaving disastrously beneath her feet, a direct result, she acknowledged miserably, of the recent close contact. Which meant she could barely trust herself either. He only had to touch her to make all her principles and resolve disappear in a puff of smoke.

And all she could do was gaze into the glitter of his golden eyes, held by them, enthralled by this inexplicable dark magic, despising herself for her weakness, her inability to fight whatever it was that drew her so disastrously to the man who had, without apparent effort, made a shambles of her whole way of life.

'Over there,' he said, in a tone of husky invitation, and his words had no meaning, no meaning at all because they didn't even ruffle the surface of a mind that was blind to everything save those magnificent, unforgettable features. And he made a sound of amused understanding, low in his throat, and reached for her shoulders, turning her gently so that she was facing the wide open windows that overlooked the Thames.

For the second time the plastic carrier slid from Chelsea's numb fingers, spilling the mangled contents

over the floor. But this time there was no embarrassment. Only pain. Searing agony that made her feel
as if her heart had been sliced from her body by a cruel,
uncaring hand.

As it had been, of course, she thought feverishly. His
hand. Was he so insensitive that he couldn't guess how
hurt she'd be? Or didn't he even care?

Sandy was sunning herself on the balcony beyond the
open windows, her long, shapely legs propped up on the
table, her lovely face half hidden by huge dark glasses,
and when Quinn called out, 'I've brought someone to
meet you,' the bare toes twitched, then wriggled, the long
limbs were hoisted to the floor and the redhead stood
up, removed the concealing sun-specs and swayed back
into the main room.

Chelsea wanted to turn and run, but she did nothing
of the kind. She would handle this encounter with
dignity, if it was the last thing she ever did.

She could see why he found the other woman totally
irresistible; the lightly tanned body was enough to send
the sanest man wild, its charm heightened, rather than
concealed, by the tiny black bikini. Chelsea closed her
eyes briefly, trying to force her frozen features back to
some semblance of normality, trying to cope with this
painful and shattering turn of events.

Quinn's hands were still resting lightly on her shoulders
and, as if from a great distance, she heard him say, 'Meet
my sister, Chelsea. It's time you were formally
introduced.'

'Hi!' Sandy wrinkled her delectable nose. 'The first
time we met I was still asleep and you were miffed. Quinn
was all set to introduce us at that charity do, but you'd

done a runner!' Suddenly, she grinned and threw back her head, lifting her riotous hair up off her shoulders. 'I've been dying to meet you; you're the first woman who's been able to give my big brother the run-around. Bully for you!'

'Scoot, brat!' Quinn jerked a thumb in the direction of the penthouse hallway. 'Make yourself scarce, and decent.'

'But I want——' Sandy began to protest, her lower lip thrust out mutinously, but Quinn cut in toughly,

'I said out, and I mean out. If you behave yourself, Chelsea and I might take you to lunch. In the meantime, go to your room and stay there. And think over what I said, and in case you decide to come down with a convenient dose of amnesia just remember that I meant every word.'

Which was enough to have the younger woman flounce out of the room heaving a dramatic sigh, and Chelsea said in a strangled voice, 'Precisely how many "sisters" do you have?'

'Two.' Quinn turned her, sliding his hands down her back, pulling the lower half of her body against his. 'And you can take that stiff, suspicious look off your face. There's Erica, who has recently presented the family tree with another twiglet, and——'

'Cassie,' Chelsea intoned firmly, fighting the rolling sensations that being so intimately near him induced.

'Cassandra,' Quinn elaborated, tightening his hands so that their bodies seemed fused together. 'A red-haired child, her name got shortened to Sandy—seemed logical.' He grinned down at her, making her heart flip. 'When she got older she hated it and decided that Cassie suited her image better. And when I had to invent a reason, off the top of my head, for my need for the engagement fiction to continue, I came up with the idea of a persistently clinging female I wanted rid of and, pushed into a corner, came up with the only "unused" name I could think of on the spur of the moment—Sandy. And the reason her childhood name presented itself must have stemmed from the fact that I've been having trouble with her for the past twelve months.'

'Trouble?' Chelsea enquired on a bright falsetto, trying her best to normalise a situation which was exactly as it shouldn't be. So the woman she'd thought he was fighting so unsuccessfully to keep out of his life was, after all, his innocent sister. But that didn't alter the fact that she shouldn't be here, in his arms, his darling proximity weakening every resolve she'd ever had. Hadn't he, only just over an hour ago, calmly told her that she could have the promotion she'd once coveted, provided . . . ?

'Trouble,' he affirmed, tilting his head and holding her unwilling gaze. 'That little sister of mine is an exuberant extrovert—a beguiling opportunist, if ever there was one. Since Ma made her home more or less permanently in Paris, Cassie decided to become uncontrollable. She's talented, believe me, and her wild antics, the crowd she mixed with, were putting her place at drama school in jeopardy. I've tried to talk some sense into her, but she's always had the knack of twisting me round her finger. Everyone knew it and so, unfortunately, did she. The night of the charity ball, she had turned up with a gang of her rowdier friends and was trying to talk me into paying a batch of particularly gruesome bills.'

Unforgivably, one of his hands rose to insert itself between their fused bodies, his fingers dealing with the buttons of Chelsea's suit jacket, his voice shamelessly husky as he told her, 'I, however, was in no mood to put up with her importunings. My mind was preoccupied with other matters.' His hand slid to the front fastening of her blouse, leaving her in no doubt about the form of those preoccupations, and she managed a strangled mew of protest, which he ignored, telling her, 'I told her to behave herself because I was about to introduce her to the woman who wore my engagement ring. But,' he amended heavily, 'we couldn't find you. You'd done a runner. Which seems to be a particularly well-perfected party piece of yours. You made me madder than a bull with a *banderilla*.' The backs of his fingers were making a gentle journey of discovery along the curving line of her lacy bra and Chelsea gulped back the emotional sob of self-disgust that was lodged in her throat. She had no control whatsoever where he was concerned and she was going to end up, briefly, in his bed, just until he tired of her, then spend the rest of her life pining for him, despising herself. She just knew it!

And, to her shame, two tears welled from her eyes, sliding down her cheeks, and she hated herself for being this weak, hated the way her mangled heart wrenched so agonisingly beneath her breasts as his hand stopped playing havoc with that part of her anatomy and lifted to carefully wipe away one crystal drop and then the other.

'It was only when you gave me that lecture about cow-ardice that everything slotted together,' he told her, the triumphant glint in his eyes making her quail. 'You kept me very determinedly at arm's length—or almost so——' he grinned unforgivably '—simply because you believed in the fictional "other woman". You were jealous!'

'And just why did you invent her?' Chelsea de-manded, taking advantage of the distraction of his amusement to fumble with the buttons he had undone, stepping back, desperately trying to put distance be-tween them because that was the only way she could cope with him.

And he let her go, his stance perfectly relaxed, very sure of himself as he shruggingly informed her, 'I had this flash of insight. You see, knowing you, your strict ethical codes, you were quite likely to change your mind about our "engagement". But I liked the idea, I really did—especially if it could be protracted. And so I came up with the mythical clinging feminine nuisance because I reckoned I knew you well enough by then to guess you would be willing, if not happy, to go along with the charade, well into the future, simply because your con-science wouldn't let you do otherwise. I had helped you out of a tight spot——'

'And I would feel duty bound to help you in return,' Chelsea interrupted raggedly, wanting to hit him for the way he had manipulated her. 'And leap into bed with you at the drop of a hat!'

'Hats weren't quite what I had in mind.' Quinn closed the distance she'd put between them, the slightest movement of his hand on her elbow depositing her on a convenient sofa, where he joined her, his hands framing her face, then tangling with her hair, releasing the pins that kept it pulled back in a controlled knot at the back of her head. 'You'd intrigued me ever since I first set eyes on you, and your request at the launch party opened doors I'd believed would need gelignite to crack.' His crooked smile melted her heart, turned it and her brain to mush. 'So, being firmly of the opinion that no man worthy of the name would ignore such an opportunity, I took every advantage of the situation.'

'Blackmailing me!' she croaked, with a praiseworthy attempt at indignation, knowing that blackmail didn't come into the equation now because she'd successfully cancelled all possibilities of that when she'd handed in her resignation.

'You didn't believe that, did you?' He was winding a strand of her silky dark hair around his finger, letting it go, only to start the process again. 'Did you really believe it was anything other than bluster? That I'd stoop to actually doing as I'd threatened?'

She had had this argument with herself before and had drawn the conclusion that no, she hadn't ever truly believed he would do that to her, or any other living soul, and she told him honestly, not meeting his eyes, 'I guess not.'

And a voice from the door to the hallway pronounced, 'I'm hungry, and decent. Is it safe to come in?'

Chelsea heard Quinn's impatient, low expletive, and he turned reluctantly, one of his hands taking one of hers in a possessive clasp.

'We'll feed you, child, provided you behave yourself in front of your future sister-in-law.'

Cassie's crow of delight was unrepentantly unsubdued, but she was wearing a skirt of sorts and a demure granny shirt which, teamed with the thigh-length tube of clinging jersey cotton, gave a definitely audacious effect. And Chelsea's poor muddled mind was still grappling with the implications of that 'future sister-in-law' all the way through a delicious lunch at Langan's, the champagne cocktails doing nothing to clear her head.

And, trying to sort out her face and her thoughts in the washroom, she was joined by Cassie, who remarked sternly, 'You are going to put the poor guy out of his misery, aren't you? He's the best brother in the world— even if he does read the Riot Act at times—and I won't see him hurt.'

'And did you take notice?' Chelsea came back, deciding to change the subject because the way in which she was supposed to put Quinn out of his misery wasn't something she wanted to discuss with this knowing young woman. And Cassie grinned, showing perfect white teeth.

'I had no option this time.' She inspected her lovely face in the mirror, grimaced slightly then heaved a sigh. 'And he's right, of course. I've been wasting time. And quite apart from his threat to withdraw all financial support, and make sure Ma did the same if I was sneaky enough to go pestering her—his words—I've got to knuckle down and work like stink if I want to make something of a career for myself. Which I do.'

Having successfully turned the younger woman's mind from Quinn's so-called misery, and the remedy for that condition, Chelsea felt the familiar weakness in her knees when Quinn put his sister in a taxi which would take her back to her own flat and hailed another to carry them back to the apartment block they shared.

Despite the champagne cocktails, she was rigid with tension. Nothing had been resolved except the true identity of the irresistible Sandy and she could get nothing straight in her mind and followed like a lamb to the slaughter when he led her into the penthouse.

As soon as the door closed behind them, he removed her suit jacket and then his own and, seemingly oblivious of her wide-eyed state, pushed her gently on to the sofa and took off her shoes, his fingers sliding erotically over her high instep, letting her curling toes and tiny accompanying gasp tell their own story.

A story he found completely satisfying, judging by the sensual curl of his mouth as he told her, 'You are never going to run out on me again. Wherever you go, I go, from now on in.' He tossed her shoes aside and removed his tie and Chelsea's mouth dried up, her heart hammering like a crazy thing. He was going to undress them both and she, weak fool that she was, knew quite well what would happen then, and could do nothing to stop it happening!

She croaked out, making one last desperate attempt to pull herself together and opt for the route of common sense against a liaison that she knew to be the path to eventual despair and loneliness, 'What do you mean by that?'

'Exactly what I say.' He had unbuttoned her blouse for the second time that day, and was sliding it off her shoulders with never a hint of a fumble, his gleaming eyes intent on hers as he stated, 'You can retract your resignation if you wish and take that promotion. If you'd stayed long enough to listen, you would have heard my conditions.' The blouse had fallen with a whisper to join their jackets, his tie and her shoes, and his eyes had dropped to the front fastening of her bra. Chelsea shuddered, fighting the temptation to help him, to unbutton his shirt, undress him completely, and his eyes met hers, as if he knew what she was thinking.

He murmured, 'As I believe I once observed, you have a direct mind. Too direct. You jump to conclusions and stick to them, even if the truth is staring you in the face.' He lifted both her hands in his, brushing his lips across her knuckles, and her voice came out sounding strangled.

'What truth?'

'That I love you.' Again the brush of his lips across the back of her captured hands. 'With hindsight, I believe it happened the first time I saw you. It was only after you'd let me know, in no certain terms, on the night of the charity ball, that you weren't about to allow me to be your lover, that I knew the truth regarding the way I felt. I walked out of your apartment practically hating you for turning me down—yet again. Read the Riot Act to Cassie—I'd insisted she return to the penthouse with me, where I could keep an eye on her and tell her a thing or two about buckling down to work and behaving herself or she'd get to know what brotherly fury really meant—and right at the end of the well-deserved tirade a slice of knowledge slipped into my mind. A calming, wonderful slice. I knew I loved you, couldn't live without you. I never thought I'd say those words to any woman again. Say them, mean them, live them.'

Tenderly, Quinn cradled her in his arms, and she clung to him as if she would never let him go, hardly able to believe that she had heard him confess the way he felt. And then he said, 'My conditions were merely that you allow me to start again in my pursuit of you. I was willing to take things as slowly as necessary—given your anti-pathy to the state of matrimony. But you walked out on me, refusing even to hear me out, and only when you revealed your jealousy of the non-existent other woman did I decide to cut a few corners. Keeping away from you these last two weeks has been hell,' he revealed soberly. 'But I knew I had to take time to get things right. I admit that my intentions weren't strictly honourable to begin with, in as much as marriage wasn't to the forefront of my mind. I had to find a way to start again, to convince you that I wanted you as a permanent fixture in my life. I had already approached Sir Leonard and the board—the acquisition was swift and painless—because I was determined to offer you all you had ever wanted as far as your career was concerned. And all I wanted in return was the opportunity to start again with you, this time to get you to trust me, to love me.'

'But I loved you all along—for what seems like forever now,' Chelsea confessed breathlessly, ecstatic joy racing through her bloodstream. She felt an answering shudder ripple strongly through Quinn's body and nuzzled her lips along the roughness of his jaw. 'And all the time I thought you were using me as a shield against——'

'A woman who didn't exist,' he finished for her, raising his head slightly as she drew a little away, her direct, slanting eyes searching his.

'You were so definite about one thing, though,' she told him slowly. 'You're not going to spend your life wondering if I married you for your money—that's if——' Suddenly she faltered, unsure again. He hadn't actually asked her, had he?

'If we are to be married?' He joined her on the sofa pulling her on to his lap, holding her close. 'You bet your sweet life we are. As I told you, you're not running out on me ever again. As I said, you may retract your resignation if you wish, or—and I admit to this being a favourite dream of mine for the past few weeks—we could make Monk's Norton our permanent home, keep this apartment for when we need to be in town, and have loads of babies. But, my darling, that's entirely up to you. And the mercenary role I threw at all women was something I once had reason to believe. And then, when Lorna was well and truly out of my system, I used it as a convenience. You see, my lovely, I never did meet a woman I could contemplate sharing my life with until I met you.'

Deftly, he released the tiny clasp at the front of her bra, his smothered groan as the removal of the lacy scrap revealed her full bounty almost sending her out of her mind. But she held on long enough to say, 'Tell me about Lorna.'

She had to know why he had kept such a cynical distrust of women for so long, and he tore his eyes from the unashamed arousal of her breasts for long enough to tell her, 'I was young, she was older. Very beautiful, polished. I didn't stand a chance. We got engaged. Then she discovered that Ryder-Gem was struggling, wasn't the gold-mine she'd believed it to be. So she broke it off and married a man old enough to be her father, but rotten rich. One of the reasons I worked as hard as I did was to make Ryder-Gem what it is today—just to show the bitch what she'd thrown away. At least, that's how it started out. Until, not too long after, I discovered that Lorna no longer entered into it. I was pulling the family firm into shape because it was a challenge I couldn't resist.' His eyes rested on the full curves of her mouth, his own softening in response. 'When I met her again she made it clear that her elderly husband had lost his charms. She knew, by then, of Ryder-Gem's financial success and lost no time in introducing the topic of divorce. Hers. And re-marriage. Ours. I looked at her and I loathed her, and from that day on I never gave her another thought. And yes, I suppose I did become something of a cynic. I knew I could buy any woman I wanted. Not that I wanted all that many——'

'What about the blondes?' Chelsea interjected at this blatant bending of the truth. 'Meryl from the coffee-shop told me you were involved with two of them—plus a redhead. But she was Sandy—Cassie—so we can discount her,' she said magnanimously, and he shook his head.

'Meryl should get her facts straight. Two blondes there were, and are. Both my secretaries. Both happily married ladies. Now, do we have to talk, and talk, and talk? There are other things I can think of——' He dipped his dark head towards her throbbing breasts, demonstrating exactly what he had on his mind, and later, so much later that the evening mist was rolling in from the river, she nuzzled closer to him in the big double bed, sliding her hands over the strong arch of his ribcage.

'About Monk's Norton, and all those babies——' And she gave a tiny squeal of ecstatic delight as Quinn rolled over, pinning her down with his magnificent body, supporting himself on his elbows as his mouth hovered a scant half-inch away from hers.

'Is that really what you want, my darling one?' And she nodded, too happy to speak, loving him so, and he smiled wickedly down at her in the soft blue light. 'Then let's make doubly sure, shall we?'

'Trebly.' Her eager body welcomed his again. 'Or quadruply, if that's a word——'

'Stop talking, witch! Can't you see I'm otherwise fully occupied . . . ?'

Relive the romance...
Harlequin® is proud to bring you

by Request™

A new collection of three complete novels every month. By the most requested authors, featuring the most requested themes.

Available in January:

WESTERN LOVING

They're ranchers, horse trainers, cowboys...
They're willing to risk their lives.
But are they willing to risk their hearts?

Three complete novels in one special collection:

RISKY PLEASURE by JoAnn Ross
VOWS OF THE HEART by Susan Fox
BY SPECIAL REQUEST by Barbara Kaye

Available wherever Harlequin books are sold.

Share the adventure—and the romance—of

HARLEQUIN ◇ PRESENTS®

A Year DOWN UNDER

If you missed any titles in this miniseries,
here's your chance to order them:

Harlequin Presents®—A Year Down Under

#11519	HEART OF THE OUTBACK by Emma Darcy	$2.89	☐
#11527	NO GENTLE SEDUCTION by Helen Bianchin	$2.89	☐
#11537	THE GOLDEN MASK by Robyn Donald	$2.89	☐
#11546	A DANGEROUS LOVER by Lindsay Armstrong	$2.89	☐
#11554	SECRET ADMIRER by Susan Napier	$2.89	☐
#11562	OUTBACK MAN by Miranda Lee	$2.99	☐
#11570	NO RISKS, NO PRIZES by Emma Darcy	$2.99	☐
#11577	THE STONE PRINCESS by Robyn Donald	$2.99	☐
#11586	AND THEN CAME MORNING by Daphne Clair	$2.99	☐
#11595	WINTER OF DREAMS by Susan Napier	$2.99	☐
#11601	RELUCTANT CAPTIVE by Helen Bianchin	$2.99	☐
#11611	SUCH DARK MAGIC by Robyn Donald	$2.99	☐

(limited quantities available on certain titles)

TOTAL AMOUNT	$
POSTAGE & HANDLING	$
($1.00 for one book, 50¢ for each additional)	
APPLICABLE TAXES*	$ _____
TOTAL PAYABLE	$ _____
(check or money order—please do not send cash)	

To order, complete this form and send it, along with a check or money order for the
total above, payable to Harlequin Books, to: *In the U.S.*: 3010 Walden Avenue,
P.O. Box 9047, Buffalo, NY 14269-9047; *In Canada*: P.O. Box 613, Fort Erie, Ontario,
L2A 5X3.

Name: _____

Address: _____City: _____

State/Prov.: _____Zip/Postal Code: _____

*New York residents remit applicable sales taxes.
Canadian residents remit applicable GST and provincial taxes.

YDUF

POSTCARDS FROM EUROPE

HARLEQUIN PRESENTS®

Hi!
Spending a year in Europe. You won't believe how great the men are! Will be visiting Greece, Italy, France and more. Wish you were here—how about joining us in January?

There's a handsome Greek just waiting to meet you.

THE ALPHA MAN
by Kay Thorpe

Harlequin Presents #1619

Available in January wherever Harlequin books are sold.

When the only time you have for yourself is...

STOLEN *moments* ™

Christmas is such a busy time—with shopping, decorating, writing cards, trimming trees, wrapping gifts....

When you do have a few *stolen moments* to call your own, treat yourself to a brand-new *short* novel. Relax with one of our Stocking Stuffers— or with all six!

Each STOLEN MOMENTS title is a complete and original contemporary romance that's the perfect length for the busy woman of the nineties! Especially at Christmas...

And they make perfect **stocking stuffers**, too! (For your mother, grandmother, daughters, friends, co-workers, neighbors, aunts, cousins—all the other women in your life!)

Look for the STOLEN MOMENTS display in December

STOCKING STUFFERS:

HIS MISTRESS Carrie Alexander
DANIEL'S DECEPTION Marie DeWitt
SNOW ANGEL Isolde Evans
THE FAMILY MAN Danielle Kelly
THE LONE WOLF Ellen Rogers
MONTANA CHRISTMAS Lynn Russell

HSM2

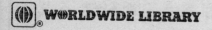

Fifty red-blooded, white-hot, true-blue hunks
from every State in the Union!

Look for MEN MADE IN AMERICA! Written by some
of our most poplar authors, these stories feature fifty of
the strongest, sexiest men, each from a different state in
the union!

Two titles available every other month at your favorite
retail outlet.

In January, look for:

DREAM COME TRUE by Ann Major (Florida)
WAY OF THE WILLOW by Linda Shaw (Georgia)

In March, look for:

TANGLED LIES by Anne Stuart (Hawaii)
ROGUE'S VALLEY by Kathleen Creighton (Idaho)

You won't be able to resist MEN MADE IN AMERICA!